MAYA'S DREAM

MAYA'S DREAM

NEDDI MITCHEL

MILL CITY PRESS

Xulon Press
2301 Lucien Way #415
Maitland, FL 32751
407.339.4217
www.xulonpress.com

Paperback ISBN-13: 978-1-66284-038-8
Ebook ISBN-13: 978-1-66284-039-5

Dedicated to my mother and my sister

If the United States is a melting pot for the world, then California is the sauté pan for the rest of the states. This Golden state, which was once the envy of North America and dream destination for just about every generation of German, Jew and Gentile including French, Swiss and Swede, is now considered the social pariah of the west coast. This sun-soaked jewel on the Pacific where orange trees and avocados grow right next to Eucalyptus and redwoods, where tans are handed out at birth and movie stars rival the common cold is now the dysfunctional family member for the "lower forty-eight." If you grew up in California, then you soon realized that there was no such thing as a "Californian" from California! Everyone was from somewhere else, Chicago, New York, Minnesota, Ohio, Detroit and Florida, yes Florida!

(You see there was a time when Florida was nothing but a big retirement home with big bugs and big lizards climbing out of the swamps while old Jews with big bucks were turning it into one great big golf course. That was before their grand children had grown up, afterwards they let amusement parks, night clubs, drugs and spring break

partying turn it into one great big hedonistic playground for the young, rich and g-stringed! But that's another state and story.)

Back on the left coast the only thing coming out of the swamp was a great big water pipe that would eventually suck the Colorado river dry and turn Palm Springs into Florida. It would turn Los Angeles into "La, La Land" and California into the produce section of the country. Only vegetables weren't the only produce it would produce! Cannabis sativa would become the boomtown bumper crop that would bring together more cultures and social opposites to the California sauté pan then the sexual revolution of the sixties, but that too is another story.

1

I t was raining on the bay, and the fog was settling in for the night. Calder was checking some leads when he glanced up from his desk just in time to notice a pair of crystal blue eyes looking back from the lobby. He noticed that the eyes also came with a pair of soft shoulders and a great pair of...

"Calder, line 3...Calder!"

"Yea, I got it,"...he answered, trying to look I'mportant., he picked up the phone and pushed it's button,

"This is Calder."

A voice on the other end was short and to the point,

"We're meeting tonight at eight."

Calder looked at his watch

That's in one hour. he thought

Calder turned his back to the office door and whispered into his phone:

"I thought I told you never to call me at…" the phone went dead.

Damn it, he thought, *I'll never make it!*

He hung up the phone and nervously began to gather his things when he remembered that he was being watched, then turned around only to find an empty lobby.

He quickly gathered up the rest of his stuff and headed out of the office.

As he entered the lobby he saw Phillip sitting there, appearing to read a magazine.

"Who was the lady?" asked Calder.

"Don't even think about it" said Phillip without looking up. "She wouldn't give you the time of day."

Phillip was a good receptionist, but he could be a smart ass sometimes.

Packed in like sardines, Calder could barely move in the elevator, which seemed to stop at every floor on the way down. Forced to stare at the side of a man's head and the forest of hair that engulfed the guy's ear, Calder could not help I'magining himself a great explorer of the Congo, chopping through the thick jungle of an ear that stared back at him. *Where's a weed whacker when you need one,* he thought to himself.

Sitting on the Bart, full of commuters as it snaked under the bay towards Berkeley, he watched a teenager with headphones on, bopping her head up and down and singing out loud while dancing in place. He looked around at the people in his car, trying to keep their balance as they came to the first stop. A man with one arm around a pole, reading the paper, a well-dressed woman with a brief case who obviously does this every day. A young man in a suit sat with a laptop open, playing computer poker. Calder looked around at all the people on his car and wondered how many of them stood like this every morning and evening on their way to and from work. He tried guessing where someone would get off by how the person was dressed. He tried to figure out how long it would be until someone would finally get home and be relaxing in front of the TV; or eating their dinner before taking a bath and going to bed so they could get up and do this all over again the next day. As he was pondering this, he noticed a fairly attractive, middle aged woman working her way through the crowded car.

Is someone going to get up and offer her their seat he wondered.

As she approached, Calder stood up to offer his seat but before he could barely clear the space the teenager slipped down in the seat and began playing drums on her legs.

"Excuse me but"... The young girl pulled her head phones off and looked up.

"What's up," the teenaged girl asked.

"Well, I was actually offering my seat to"... he looked around only to see the back of the woman as she headed to the next car.

"That's twice" he thought.

He turned back to the teenager who was gyrating in her seat and...

"IT'S NOT MY FAULT, A FATAL ERROR HAS OCCURRED! NOT ENOUGH MEMORY. PLEASE SAVE ALL INFORMATION ON BACK UP DISC AND RESTART COMPUTER."

"Shit!" said Maya
"What" said Paul
"Fatal fucking error! That's what"
"Did you save it." Asked Paul
"I didn't have time"
"Well just hit restart and" ...
"I can't it's frozen" screamed Maya
"Well hit control, option and escape at the same" ...
"I know what to do Paul, I'm just sick of having to do it all the fucking time!"
"Maya, quit cussing and come to bed." Said Paul.

2

D o you ever wake up early in the morning, but you don't actually wake up? You slowly come out of your sleep, but you don't open your eyes? When this happens, you can sometimes actually feel your body relaxing in your bed. You can feel the weight of your body sinking into the mattress. You can hear subtle sounds around you, but they don't really register. Maya was having one of those mornings and it was wonderful.

She could feel every contour and curve that her body made in the futon. She could actually feel gravity working as it gently pulled her head down into her pillow. She could smell the clean cotton off the pillowcase. She could hear the faint sound of birds outside and the wind blowing as a car started in the distance. She could also hear Paul breathing in bed next to her. She could feel his warm breath on the side of her neck and his knees slightly brushing against her thigh. She could smell his familiar sent which felt comforting and she slowly rolled onto her side and let her arm come to rest on his chest. As she took in a deep breath through her nose and gently caressed the little patch of smooth hair on Paul's chest, she slowly opened her eyes and almost went into shock. Who in the hell was this stranger in her bed! She pulled her head back and took a second look. Who the hell are you? "She thought." She knew that it really was Paul, so she didn't jump from the bed, but it looked nothing like him. He looked like a complete stranger.

Have you ever awoken early in the morning and looked at the same person you have known for years, shared the same bed with, seen the face you've seen a million times but suddenly for some reason they look completely different? Well Maya was having one of those mornings and it was bizarre.

Maybe it was the dl'm light of the morning coming through the frosted windows. Perhaps it was that she was looking at the strange shadows on his face too close, but as she was lying there looking at Paul, she couldn't help but think how strange he looked, and it was spooky. She did'nt recognize his face.

She remembered three years ago, when he tripped over Parker's bike in the garage and broke his nose;

and she thought what a great job the doctor did of straightening it out.

"It looks just fine" she reassured Paul.

You could hardly notice any difference. Yet this morning as she looked at him, his nose looked deformed making his eyes look uneven. Who is this freak? She laughed to herself.

As she studied the tiny scar on his forehead that now looked to her like a giant canyon in his face, he opened his eyes. Maya almost jumped out of her skin!

"God dang it, don't do that," she said as she slapped his chest.

"What?" Asked Paul.

"You scared the shit out of me," said Maya; reaching for her bottle of water.

"Well how was I to know you'd be right there in my face, I was just opening my eyes and waking up, I didn't know that you'd be ..." Paul began to say.

He stopped speaking after noticing how Maya was looking at him.

"What?" Paul stared back. "What?" he said louder.

"Sometimes you're one freaky looking thing in the morning," said Maya.

Paul got up and headed for the bathroom.

"Funny, that's what they said about you at San Jose State."

"Who?" said Maya.

"The football team," said Paul.

Quickly closing the bathroom door as Maya threw a pillow at him.

"Ha, ha, ha," said Maya, "Well at least I got laid in college!"

"Least is the last word I would use to describe your college sex life," said Paul, through the door.

"Well, it seems to apply to our sex life now," said Maya as she went to pick up the pillow from in front of the door.

"Were not in college anymore, Maya," said Paul. "We can't fuck every night."

Maya leaned into the door and softly shouted, "I can, but even once or twice a week would be nice."

"What would be nice?" asked a soft voice from behind Maya.

Maya turned around to see Parker standing in the doorway, half-asleep in his tee shirt and underwear; scratching his butt.

"What would be nice once or twice a week?" repeated Parker.

"A walk," said Maya as she leaned over and kissed the top of his head.

"Mommy would like to take a walk every night." Maya to Parker.

She put her arm around him and started walking towards the kitchen. As they headed down the hall she leaned back and shouted loudly towards the bedroom,

"But once or twice a week would be nice!"

Then turning back to Parker...she asked,

"What do you want for breakfast?"

"Cheerios?" Parker begged.

"OK, And what about your brother? "Maya continued.

"He wants waffles. " Parker answered

"Oh, he does, does he? Well, he'll have to get out here and help me."

Just as the words left her mouth, they walked into the kitchen to see that Eli had already found the flour and had it all over himself and the kitchen counter!

"Wafoos" said Eli looking up at Parker and Maya.

"We have frozen ones" exclal'med Parker

"Fowzen ones?" continued Eli.

"Yes, fowzen wafoos, there in the fridge," said Maya.

"Where's Carrie-Anne?" Maya asked.

"She's still upstairs, probably on the computer," said Parker.

Maya brushed some flour off Eli's arm and walked towards the stairs, to call up to Carrie-Anne. Her bedroom was over the garage. They had added it on to their sl'mple farm style home as a studio for Maya before they started a family. But by the time Carrie-Anne was ten years old; Maya was too busy with the kids to write, and Carrie-Anne needed her own room. It was connected to the main house by stairs that came down into the living room where the hallway began. Just as Maya reached the point where the hallway met the stairs Paul came walking out as Maya was about to shout up to Carrie-Anne. Startled, Maya jumped slightly.

"Jesus" said Maya.

"What now!" said Paul.

"Don't do that, damn it!" Maya pleaded.

"What'd I do now" Paul asked.

"Sneaking up on me like that!" Maya answered. "I didn't sneak up on you. " Giggled Paul, as he tried to dodge her swat at his butt.

"Then why are you laughing?" Maya demanded.

"I'm not laughing," said Paul as he headed into the kitchen, "it's just that you're always so damn jumpy."

"I'll give you something to jump about!" Cracked Maya, as she headed back to the stairs.

"Carrie-Ann are you coming down or what" Maya demanded.

Returning to the kitchen she saw Paul and Eli cleaning up the mess on the floor. Taking her favorite mug from its place on the windowsill, she poured herself a cup of coffee.

"You want a cup?" She asked Paul

"Yea, sure." Paul answered.

Maya handed him a cup and sweetly kissed him on his lips "Good morning," she mumbled.

"Morning," he replied.

He held the cup in one hand and the small of her back in the other and pulled her close for another kiss.

As they embraced, he let his hand slip down onto her butt, it was promptly but playfully slapped off.

"You had your chance last night Romeo." snipped Maya.

Maya, Parker and Eli began giggling as Maya pulled away and headed for the porch to get the paper.

"What's so funny?" asked Paul teasingly.

The boys broke into full-blown laughter as Paul watched Maya glide out of the kitchen and float towards the front door.

Gliding or floating would be the best way to describe how Maya moved. She had fluidity in her gait, looking as if she were dancing when she walked. She had taken ballet lessons for several years when she was young and was also on the gymnastics team and ran track in high school. The genetic gods must have been drunk the day she was conceived, because they had given the best genes to her. She got the best of both her parent's strongest features. She had her mother's silk skin and stunning beauty and the well-defined lines of her father. And although she was only 5'-6" she was all legs, and in heels she looked like a runway model with muscles. The gal was a looker!

Despite winter's grasp, the morning looked promising. Clouds spread across the sky but had their hands full fighting back the sun as it peeked through the gaps.

Although it was still a bit chilly, the cold wet cement under Maya's feet it felt good, while she bent down to get the paper.

Looks like a great day, she thought.

She plopped herself down on the porch and glanced at the paper while slurping her coffee. As she studied the front page, she could here Eli and Josh fighting over the waffles. Nemo popped out of the shrubs and slipped under Maya's knee and started rubbing against her leg.

"Morning Nemo," said Maya.

The cat meowed and crawled around Maya's legs. Nemo was cool grey with white cuffs and a black spot on the end of his tail.

"I'll feed you in a sec, "said Maya "just chill, ok"

Maya went back to reading her paper, and Nemo crawled into her lap to take in the morning. Nemo was once the neighbor's cat. He originally belonged to Mrs. Namaguchi. When Mrs. Namaguchi died, her son offered Maya the cat he moved to Arizona...And that was that.

Maya looked at the front page of the paper. There was an article with an accompanying letter from the Mayor. Apparently, the Mayor had been caught dumping a stack of newspapers that contained an article exposing him in a situation contrary to the life-style he had clal'med to perpetuate. The Mayor had been elected on a platform that encouraged support of the community and the local organic farmers and dairymen, whose products promoted his vegan way of life. The article which he had been trying to keep from the eyes of the community, had been published by a small neighborhood paper. It displayed photos of the Mayor shopping at a Safeway market, buying pesticide laden grapefruit from Texas, along with a quart of whole milk and some I'mported German chocolate. "Our Vegan is a Regan!" the headline clal'med. "Ghirardelli chocolate not good enough for Mayor!"

The article went on to expose other items in the Mayor's shopping cart, all were strictly I'mports to the bay area. In a state of panic and fearful of retribution, the Mayor thought he could destroy the evidence soon enough to come up with a defense for his actions. This defense was in a letter that was on the front page of the paper now sitting softly on Maya's lap. The mayor's said that he was sl'mply tying to appease his stressed and frantic wife who was eight months pregnant, having extreme urges for grapefruit and a chocolate syrup milkshake!

Maya read on as the article explained, that even though Ghirardelli chocolate had been started by an emigrant family from Germany, its birth was in San Francisco and was as much a part on California *as "San Francisco Sourdough bread." And that even though they called the grapefruit "Texas Ruby Reds" they were prl'marily grown and harvested in Mexico by starving children working in the fields of Oaxaca; and that the Mayor was supporting child slavery, the German economy and anthrax in cattle! Maya almost spit coffee through her nose as she tried to stop from laughing. She had a sense of humor that had no boundaries and the story in the paper was an easy excuse to indulge it.*

3

Maya had been born on a commune in Big Sur to Darnell and Yolanda Williams. The two had fled Los Angeles where they had been politically active protesting the war in Vietnam. Darnell was a black man who grew up in LA and Yolanda, a black/French woman born outside of Paris in Agier. Yolanda moved to Los Angeles after high school and lived with her aunt. She wanted to see the US. and that's where she met Darnell. He was a studio musician who worked for various artists, but also did silk screening and made posters for small militant groups that were promoting the civil rights movement. They fell in love and moved to San Francisco; where they became consumed by the "summer of love" as well as each other. But after a couple encounters with law enforcement and a notice from draft board, Darnell decided he needed a safer place of haven for himself and his new bride. They found out about a commune in the mountains of Bid Sur; and Maya was born shortly there after. But communal life in the woods soon grew old for Yolanda. She was pregnant again and was tired of living in the same compound with four other families. She was tired of bathing in a river and surviving on a vegetarian diet. So, after Darnell served his time for desertion, they settled in Santa Cruz where he used his poster making skills to open a silkscreen shop and Yolanda now had bathtub and a good steak.

Yolanda would have two more girls and then finish two more years of classes at Cabrillo College to get her certificate in dental hygiene. She worked for a practice in Redwood City. The commute was tough, but when Darnell won a contract screening t-shirts and sweats for "Ganja Surf Ware of Santa Cruz" he made enough money to sell his silkscreen business and with a small loan from the bank, they moved their four daughters to a little place in Palo Alto where Darnell started a small printing company. They would go on to have two more boys.

Although still politically active, Yolanda and Darnell channeled their energy into their community keeping a low profile. They had no desire to disturb the comfortable nest they had built for their family. The same could not be said for Maya.

Maya was a strange and rebellious fruit from day one. She entered the world a breech baby, umbilical cord wrapped around her neck. She should have choked to death, but she had begun chewing on the cord at eight months in the womb. So, when she came out it was feet first, the cord in her mouth; the cord snapped in two as she twisted her head around to look at her mother. Plopping into the waiting palms of her father, Maya screamed at the top of her lungs. She tried sitting up, then struggled frantically to free herself from Darnell's grasp! That would be the first of many acts of defiance that would follow.

As a little girl, up until she was seven years old, Maya would run around the house and the yard naked as a jaybird. She got into her first fight when she was in the second grade, because another kid looked at her the wrong way.

"What'd she say?" asked her mom.

"Nothing" replied Maya, "it was the way she just looked at me"

"Well what way did she look at you"?

"The wrong way"! said Maya.

She was reprl'manded in junior high for painting the United Farm Workers logo on several walls at school. Although her parents supported her convictions in what she believed in, they insisted she scrub the walls clean as well as the side of their house and Darnel's truck, which had also become a billboard for Maya's artistic forms of expression. At fourteen she broke her leg trying to jump over a car riding a skateboard. The one consolation her mother had was the fact that Maya's brothers and sisters seemed to learn from her mistakes. Not that Maya didn't try to corral her siblings into her ring of wild behavior. But after trying to get them to jump off the roof with umbrellas, assuring them they would float down to earth unharmed; they sat in the waiting room of the hospital while she got six stitched in her forehead, and swore never to listen to her again. But It didn't seem to matter to Maya if they joined in her antics or not, by the time she entered high school; she had her own small group of doters that hung on her every word.

When she was sixteen she and her buddies ran across the football field in the buff during the home-coming game with paper bags over their heads. They would've gotten away scott free, except for the United Farm Workers logo painted on their butts! They were arrested at school the next day for indecent exposure. This of course brought them temporary star status from the rest of the student body.

Maya's parents on the other hand were not as Impressed. Although they would re-tell the story with admiration and laughter for the rest of their lives, when Maya finally graduated from high school and went off to San Jose State, her parents were sad to see her go, but were looking forward to a break in the actions of Maya's wildness.

It took Maya five years to graduate from college, yet she made the Dean's list. In fact, she would be the first one to tell you she's not sure what she learned from college. Though there were rumors she actually "taught" a few classes of her own when she was there...

Sex Education 101:
This class was always full and always in session.
Drinking and party 101B:
If you didn't pass out, you didn't pass!

4

After reading the paper, Maya walked back into the house to find Paul watching a fishing show holding a waffle in his hand. Tossing him the paper, she noticed Carrie-Anne in the kitchen in Paul's old baseball jersey drinking milk from the carton.

"Nice of you to finally join us," said Maya

"Morning," mumbled Carrie-Anne as she quickly put down the milk carton and reached for a glass from the cupboard.

A loud, beat up Mustang pumping out loud music pulled onto their lawn. Although it had dents everywhere and spackled paint spots with a cracked windshield, it sported a set of chrome rl'ms that were so bright it almost hurt your eyes to look at them.

A tall, lanky, dark young man in a handsome, silk shirt stepped out of the car and started strolling up the lawn. He wore a pair of clean baggy denl'ms, and a New York Yankees baseball cap. Carrie-Anne ran to the kitchen window.

"Hey, Rollow, what up?" Carrie-Anne asked.

As Carrie–Anne leaned out over the sink, Maya suddenly realized that Paul's old baseball jersey was literally all Carrie-Anne had on. Stepping quickly too the window she pinched Carrie-Anne on her bare butt.

"Ouch," chirped Carrie-Anne as she pulled away.

"Go get some clothes on young lady," ordered Maya, rolling her eyes. Carrie-Anne darted back upstairs as Maya spun around to intercept Rollow at the window.

"Morning, Rollow," said Maya

"Morning, Mrs. McKenna" replied the young man, trying to look over her shoulder and catch a gll'mpse of Carrie-Anne running up the stairs.

Briefly, the two shifted from side to side as Maya tried to block his sight line to her daughter while Rollow tried to maneuver to get a better look.

"Would you like some breakfast" Asked Maya

"No thanks I'm coo, I just came to pick up Carrie-Anne," Rollow answered.

"Oh" said Maya, you two taking the boys to the "Y"?

"The "Y"?, Rollow asked.

21

Maya saw the puzzled look on Rollow's face.

"Come on in a sec," said Maya.

Rollow walking to the porch, let himself in the front door. He could smell coffee and waffles as he stepped around the legos, hot wheels and other toys scattered all over the floor. Paul was on the sofa with his coffee watching TV.

"Hey Rollow," said Paul, "want some Joe?"

"Naw I'm coo.

He stood there for a moment while Maya headed to the bottom of the stairs and called up to Carrie-Anne.

"Carrie-Anne! Did you forget your brothers have their swI'm lessons today"?

After a moment of silence, a dejected Carrie-Anne sauntered out of her room, stood at the top of the stairs,and looked down at he mother

"Oh mom, do I have..."

"Yes, you do, we talked about this, I need to get some writing done today and just as I'mportant" Maya answered as she started up the stairs, "you need to spend some time with your brothers."

Carrie-Anne met her at the top of the stairs in jeans and a leopard bra.

"Nice bra," said Maya softly as she pushed Carrie-Anne back into the bedroom and closed the door.

Rollow slumped down in a chair next to Paul.

"Look at that bass!" said Paul

"Yea, coo," mumbled Rollow half-heartedly.

An awkward silence fell over the living room, for the moment as the two men stared at the TV, watching a man in a boat on a lake in the rain with a pole in his hand. Paul got up and headed for the kitchen, asking Rollow,

"You want a waffle or something, maybe some juice"

"No, I'm coo," Rollow answered.

Paul entered the kitchen where the two boys were sitting at the table.

"Wut up gee?" exclal'med Paul.

The two boys looked at their dad as if he was speaking a foreign language. Paul laughed.

"Why don't you two go get your swl'm shorts on and get ready for your lesson."

Twenty minutes later Carrie-Anne, Rollow and the two boys were cll'mbing into Rollow's Mustang. He was playing with the two boys as he helped them into the back seat. He was accustomed to the fact the sometimes Carrie-Ann's younger brothers were part of the deal when he wanted to see her and that was "coo" with him. An extra twenty dollars and an OK to hit the mall on the way home, had Carrie-Anne in a better mood as well.

"What are we going to do with that girl"? asked Maya.

Paul turned toward the house, "what do you mean we?"

There was one half of a famous comedy duo that sang a somewhat popular song long after his partner had passed. In the song he lamented about how he wished he were eighteen again. Of course, he was eighty-four at the time and had been overheard forty years earlier saying he was having the time of his life and wouldn't want to go back to being a teenager for all the bamboo in Bali.

It's amazing how our reflections on life can change as the years go by. There is that fickle time in a person's life when one part of you feels overwhelmed by the responsibilities of being an adult and you crave for the sI'mple care- free days of a teenager. Those days, when your existence (although not necessarily your happiness) was provided by other adults. And yet there is a time in your life when you reflect on the past with appreciation and envy, but not necessarily desire.

There was also a popular British crooner that once belted out how he wished that as a teenager, he knew the things he had learned later in life. Not exactly a revelation when it comes to epiphanies, but as they say, hindsight is 20-20.

It's one thing to wish for the days of youth with all its freedom from responsibility and the excitement of the looming future. But if at seventeen, we were to know of the perils and obstacles that lay before us in life, it could well ruin those care-free days of desire and dreams. When life becomes finding a job after college, then finding our lifelong partner only to have our heart broken. Then repeating this process again and again in the search for happiness, one's emotional strings can become frayed. As we struggle with the reality of going from one job to the next, achieving success, and then experiencing failure. Hitting a peak, and thinking this is finally it, only to come crashing down and having to start all over. Eventually the shine starts to fade on that brass ring we're reaching for. This type of life experience can become the roots of a tree that branches into a midlife crisis.

It can be said that these peaks and valleys are what makes life the wonderful ride that it is. Or as a Hallmark card might say, "The joys of strife make up the fiber and character which makes each individual's life unique and special." As schmaltzy as that might sound, there may be truth in those words. But let's face it, if we knew what the real world had in store for us once we got out of college, we would never want to finish school. In fact, the term "Career student" could be listed as a major at most universities. Yet for some teenagers, there is no pre-set agenda for them after high school. It might be because of the high cost of a college education, but in the United States there are plenty of options with Junior colleges and financial aid. For a lot of parents, they are sI'mply satisfied with the fact that they got their little monster through high school in the first place!

Neither scenario was the case for Carrie-Ann McKenna. She was fortunate enough to have two parents who, although weren't rich, could afford to send her to any local college or state university in the country. And Carrie-Ann had the grades to back up her parents' dollars. But they weren't in any rush to send their daughter off to college before she knew what she wanted to study. Having that cushion of support, she had burst through the front doors of her high school on the last day of her senior year and tore off her shirt, and screamed at the top of her lungs,shouting:

"Free at last, free at last, thank God all mighty I'm free at last"

Not exactly what Martin Luther King Jr. had in mind in his historical speech. But perhaps even the reverend himself would've enjoyed the sight of an elated young woman in the back of a car with her girlfriends driving away from high school for the last time, even if she was half naked!

5

As their kids drove away with Rollow, Paul returned to his fishing show; and Maya poured herself another cup of coffee. She took a sip and looked over at Paul in front of the TV and thought how much he looked like Eli. She suddenly realized how much he was actually just like Eli, sI'mple, silly and satisfied in his own little world. She remembered early that morning and the strange man she saw in her bed. She thought about their days in college when they first met and how things had come to pass.

She had developed a theory about her and Paul. She felt that when you meet someone who possesses the qualities you wish you had, usually one of two things happens. The two of you become close friends or your envy gets in the way of appreciation. Sometimes that quality you wished to possess is not really a good quality, but it's fun and reckless and your attraction to this type of behavior allows you to vicariously live out your true desires through this person. Hence, our obsession with the anti-hero, who can spit in the face of convention for all of us. We are all attracted in some way if not strongly to our personal opposite. And when the two meet it either creates a connection made in the cosmos, which is as rare as a white buffalo, or it sparks love/hate tendencies strong enough to create a schizophrenic relationship. But usually, when people with opposite personalities collide, the result is the opposite of what should happen. When opposite energies hit the dance floor, they usually don't want to share the same space, like positive and negative magnets they repel each other. But for some reason with humans, a fire and ice relationship can create a festive cocktail. Yet the hangover is usually waiting down the road. But don't try to tell this to the rich girl from the nice neighborhood and the poor boy from the wrong side of the tracks. The more he tells her,

"Find someone else. I'm no good for ya."

The more she cries to her father,

"But Daddy, I love him!"

This classic scenario, which has been played out on the big screen in numerous films over the years, *rolled out its red carpet when she met Paul. Although neither of them grew up rich, you could hardly call them poor, and there were no tracks within ten miles of their neighborhoods. Still, their individual experiences growing up hardly made their marriage a lock in Vegas. He was well mannered and somewhat regl'mented. She was a loose cannon.*

{Paul McKenna}

Paul was raised an only, child more or less. He had a brother Dexter; ten years older than he was, but when Paul was five his folks split up, and he only saw Dexter once or twice a year. Although cordial with each other as adults, they were more like distant friends rather than like brothers; barely managing to get together every other Christmas. His Father and stepmother, who were also opposites couldn't help but raise him on a steady diet of mixed messages. His father pushed him for excellence with well defined borders and his stepmom coddled him yet gave him plenty of rope.

"Finish what you start," his dad would say. "No one likes a half ass job."

But with his stepmom it was,

"Oh, that's close enough, no need to guild the lily."

So, at eighteen years old, Paul was a young man of many talents and a gifted athlete. But his lack of motivation and fear of success kept him from pursuing lofty goals. He was offered a football scholarship at Arizona State, but after watching a quarterback have his leg torn from his body on Monday night football he decided to pass, no pun intended!

"But you're passing up a college education," preached his father.

Instead, Paul took an offer in Sarasota with a professional baseball team. It was his first summer after high school and he was free, he had money, and he was being paid to play baseball. He was in heaven. But in Sarasota he was so homesick, he couldn't eat and lost fifteen pounds. One night he just left the team hotel at 11pm and caught the red eye flight for the west coast. When he called his parents from the airport his stepmom said...

"Oh, I'm so glad you're home and safe."
"What the hell!" screamed his father.

After arguing for twenty minutes on the phone, his father agreed to send him a cab. But less than half an hour later, his stepmom drove up in her station wagon.

Paul worked at his father's hardware store for the next two years. He listened to his dad whine about how he had thrown away a career in the big leagues. He tried to explain to his dad that he was a third string pitcher on a triple-A ball club and his chances of making the team were slim at best. Once his dad accepted the fact that he would not be living out his own dreams of playing professional baseball through his son, he realized the potential for Paul in the hardware business. Unfortunately, "McKenna and Sons" were not in Paul's plans.

As a kid he loved going to the store with his dad. Running the cash register, stocking the tools and sorting the nuts and bolts and putting them in their proper place by size and shape. But by the time he was thirteen, the job had lost some of its luster. Then again, by that time he was actually getting paid and making some money, which was hard to beat. He even started to appreciate his father's philosophy, use the right tool for the right job, a place for everything and everything in its place! After a year at the hardware store working with his dad, he realized that he was being groomed to take over the family business. So, he applied to San Jose State, and began his studies as a history major.

"Well, that's just fine!" said his dad,"When I want you to go to college, you want to play baseball. And when I want you to play baseball, you want to go to college!"

"That's just wonderful," beamed his stepmom, "Now you can go to school and live here at home with us."

Once again, Paul had other plans. He decided to live on campus where he could enjoy the complete college experience and focus on his studies, show a commitment to getting an education. Less then two years later he would drop out, but not before meeting a young black woman named Maya Williams. She was an English major. And she was as beautiful as she was wild. And of course... she was his opposite!

Maya came out of her thoughts and looked around. A box of frozen waffles sat on the counter next to a bottle of syrup and an open carton of milk. The floor was covered with toys clothes and scraps of food.

"I'm leaving the kitchen for you," she shouted as she disappeared into the bedroom to do some writing at the computer.

Paul mumbled something and settled down in front of an eight-pound bass that was being pulled out of a frozen lake on the TV screen.

People back east don't want to hear about winter in California, Hell, they come out west in December to vacation and get away from their frost bite, frozen roads, shovel the driveway and scrape the ice off the wings "real winter" they have every year. They tell jokes about how all the movie stars in LA suddenly loose control of their cars as soon as a little rain hits

the streets. Yet the effect on a city and its people during the winter is all relative. When it's gray and wet and you're cold, it doesn't matter to you if it's fifty degrees or twenty degrees, you're uncomfortable. You don't want to be outside, and when you are, you don't want to stop and talk, you keep your head down and keep moving. Everything seems to take longer, and people get I'mpatient and depressed. It's a known fact that the suicide rate goes up across the country every winter. A city's disposition in the winter is a stark contrast to its people and their behavior during the summer months, and the Bay area is no different. When January comes around, everyone is broke after the holidays and no one has seen the sun in weeks. The Golden Gate Bridge hides in the fog and gets moody. The rain clouds continue to drench the streets until the 101 gets flooded and snorkels its way north to Marin, Berkeley starts barking at Oakland who doesn't want to hear it and San Francisco is down right pissed.

6

A wet wind hit Calder right in the face as he ascended the stairs from the Bart station. Momentarily disoriented, he looked around, got his bearings before heading down Shattuck Avenue towards the bath-houses. Looking at the clock on the Wells Fargo bank he saw that he was cutting it close. Water splashed from under his wingtips, as he made his way through the gauntlet of people on the street. They all seemed to be heading in the opposite direction and he had to constantly dodge people to get out of their way.

When he was in the fifth grade, he went on a field trip to the aquarium with his school. There was a big round fish tank filled with silver mackerel. You walked up inside the tank as the fish swI'm around you in a circle. Hundreds of shinny silver bodies with big eyes swI'mming all around him in the same direction made Calder dizzy. He then noticed that there were a few fish that were swI'mming in the opposite direction than the rest of the school. They looked lost and confused as they bounced off the walls of the tank trying to avoid all the fish going the other way. That's how Calder felt now, as he traversed the people on the street. Like a salmon heading the wrong way during the spawn.

As he approached the next corner, he saw a car stuck in the intersection. An old man in a turban was behind the wheel and had committed the cardinal sin in city traffic. He had tried to make a left turn but had been too slow on the gas and when the light changed, he got stuck half way into the intersection. He couldn't go forward because of the cars moving through the intersection coming from his right, and he was blocking the cross traffic coming from the left. To make things worse, he couldn't back up because people were already crossing the street behind his car. The poor old sod was in no man's land. Calder wondered why the people didn't just stop crossing the street behind his car for one second so the poor guy could back up. As Calder approached the curb, he paused for a second hoping others would follow his lead, but that just added to the congestion as people tried to walk around him to cross the intersection.

"What has society come to?" he thought. "Is everyone so damn busy that they can't spare two little minutes out of their terribly precious and I'mportant lives to help this guy out of a jam? I guess they all have places to go and people to see and have no time or patience for the distractions of an old man stuck in traffic!"

As they crossed the street in their wet coats, they seemed to resemble that shinny school of mackerel, oblivious to the world around them. The whole scene made Calder sick as he crossed behind the old man in his car with horns honking and people yelling. He slipped through the crowd, past the bathhouse and ducked into "The Long-Life Tofu Palace."

Now one would think that a warm restaurant smelling of hot broth and Chinese dumplings would be a welcomed segue from the rain and cold of the crowded streets outside. Yet the noise inside the "The Long-Life" seemed to rival if not eclipse the chaotic din from the city outside. The clinking of knives and forks on plates, the clacking of chop sticks on bamboo bowls, the banging of pots and pans in the back round while two cooks argued in the kitchen as a chef shouted over the loud music that an order was ready. Two waiters were yelling back and forth in Chinese as the soup was slurped; the wonton crunched, while the egg foo young got older every minute. It seemed like every jaw was chewing on something yet everyone in the place was talking to each other all at once, every damn mouth in the whole damn place was moving!

Calder stood there a moment and looked around the packed room until a man stood up at the far end of the restaurant, it was Isaac Copeland, and he was waving him over. Once again, he found himself maneuvering through what seemed like throngs of people and chairs and faces until he was finally able to sit down and catch his breath.

Isaac was sitting with two men and Calder recognized them both although he thought he had only met one of them once before. That's because Chaz and Harlan Zakorsky were identical twins, or so it seemed.

Isaac stuck out his hand.

"Hey Calder, thanks for coming, you remember Chaz Zakorsky?"

"Of course" replied Calder as they shook hands "The Headlands protest, last summer right?"

"That's right" replied Chaz

"You're late" spouted Harlan

"This is his brother Harlan" Isaac slipped in.

"Well, I came straight from work, and the traffic and rain slowed everything down."

"Well that's kind of why we're here isn't it" said Isaac, "want some sweet and sour soup?"

"I thought it was hot and spicy?" said Harlan

"You're thinking of sweet and spicy" said Chaz

"You mean sour and spicy," said Harlan

"No, I don't think so" said Chaz "I think what you mean is..."

"Don't tell me what I mean" snapped Harlan

"Would you like some soup?" asked Isaac

"That'd be great!" said Calder.

Isaac waved his hand in the air to flag a waiter as Chaz and Harlan continued their debate.

"Why would they make a hot *and* spicy soup"? asked Chaz, "you want a contrast in flavors"

"Contrast my ass," spewed Harlan "you've been watching too much damn "Food TV!"

Like most Chinese restaurants it took less then two seconds for a waiter to appear with a hot bowl of sweet and sour soup.

"Can we get another menu"? Harlan asked the waiter.

"I didn't realize you had a twin" said Calder.

"We're not twins," snipped Harlan without looking up from the menu."He's my older brother by two and a half years."

Calder found this very hard to believe, as would anybody else looking at the two men who seemed completely identical. Aside from both men possessing the same short and slinky build, they each had chalk white hair with the same short cut. Both men sported white bottle brush beards to go with their matching hair. Their faces shared not only the same mouth, nose and crystal blue eyes, but they each had age lines in the same places on their faces. To add a strange twist to this mix, both men had the same little dark red apple shaped birthmarks on the same side of their necks. The two brothers had grown up working in the steel factories and lumber camps and both had massive fore arms that contrasted their relatively skinny biceps. I'm telling you, if you stuck a corncob pipe in their mouths, you'd be looking at Popeye's pappy times two! Harlan tossing the menu into the middle of the table faced Calder, saying,

"What'd I tell ya?"

Calder looked down at the menu and sure enough, the restaurant served...

Hot and sour soup!
Sweet and sour soup!
Sour and spicy soup!
And Hot and spicy soup!

"Quite a variety," said Calder. "I didn't realize they served so many types of..."

"What's the point" interrupted Harlan, "the people running this restaurant are like the people running this city, and this country mind you. They want everyone to feel like they should be able to have whatever they want. What's wrong with egg flower soup? That's what all the Chinese restaurants served when I was a kid, and no one complained then. But today everyone wants a choice. Hell, I was in the market the other day and they had fifteen types of eggplant, can you believe that, fifteen! Do we really need fifteen different types of friggin eggplant!"

Calder wasn't sure what to say

"Look" said Chaz, "the idea of giving everyone what they want is fine when you're talking about varieties of soup or vegetables" glaring at Harlan, he added. "But you can't do that when it comes to running a city."

Isaac joined in, "You can't please everyone."

"It's not healthy" chimed Harlan

"That type of thinking" continued Chaz, "creates a society of spoiled people who feel they should have a say about everything."

"Look," said Harlan, piping in again like a back up singer, "everyone is entitled to they're opinion, as long as they keep it to themselves!"

The conversation was now getting Isaac's juice flowing, And he leaned in closer to Calder like a secret agent sharing classified information.

"This system is becoming mutated my friend" he whispered.

Isaac Copeland had graduated from Berkeley with a degree in Cultural Behavior after growing up in the Silicon Valley. Both his parents were original members of the TI'mothy Leary psychedelic social club in the days when the hippies ruled Hollywood. They eventually moved up to Los Gatos and became computer designers. After college Isaac repaired computers by trade, but also free-lanced commentary for "the Berkeley Voice," a local community paper whose opinion and policies he did not always favor, but their checks never bounced, and they gave him the freedom to spout his views. He was spirited and had his opinions, and right now, over a bowl of hot and spicy, his highly stI'mulated and analytical mind was starting to churn on all cylinders.

"Do you realize how long it takes this town to make sI'mple every day decision like sI'mply putting in a fucking stop light? Did you follow what happened after the "Glady Incident?" Isaac said angrily.

"Ludicrous!" mumbled Harlan shaking his head.

Isaac continued, "First, there was the usual bureaucratic banter where it was determined that the city now needs a new traffic light at some corner so that the elderly can cross the street safely. Then someone makes a proposal, then it's presented to the city council, then they vote on it. But before it can be I'mplemented the community decides it should have a voice in the decision because someone felt that this traffic light would divert work commuters through their neighborhood and that would create needless traffic passing through a school zone and therefore endanger children that are getting out of class. So, what do they do? They have another meeting with the city council and debate the pros, cons and options, which takes another five months."

"It was ridiculous!" chirped Harlan.

Isaac was starting to roll now, he continued, "when the city finally decides to put in the light, the Urban League accuses the city of making too much money off street maintenance work going on around the city and that an independent company should get the contract. So, trying to please everyone, the city awards the job to a small company in Oakland. But when an electrical contractor who lives on the same street where this light is going in, finds out that not only was his bid the lowest and that the company who won the contract is from another city, he takes Berkeley to court and tries to sue the city for nonsupport. When he loses, he is so distraught that he goes out to that corner on the first day they install the new light, waits for it to turn green and throws himself in front of a passing bus."

"Are you kidding me?" responded Calder

"I wish I were," answered Isaac.

"You want some moo shoo pork?" Isaac asked.

"Do I want some what? oh, uh, yea sure I guess," answered Calder.

"Tempheh, tofu or seitan? Isaac continued.

"What do you mean?" Questioned Calder.

"They don't use real meat in this restaurant, so the moo shoo pork isn't actually pork. It's a meat substitute." said Isaac

"But of course, here in Berkeley" chides Harlan, "you have a choice of what you want that meat substitute to be"

"Tempheh, tofu, or seitan" repeats Isaac
"Uh, I'll have whatever you're having," said Calder
 Isaac raises his hand again and calls to the waiter,
"Moo shoo pork!"

✳ The "Glady Incident" ✳
As traffic, and the time to get where you needed to be moved further away from each other, motorist and pedestrians in the Bay area did the exact opposite. People walking down the street stopped stopping for red lights at intersections, and people in cars stopped stopping for the people who stopped stopping for red lights at intersections! Within a few months the number of people getting hit by cars had surpassed the totals for the previous year!

So, the city council, after numerous meetings with city planners as well as environmentalists who presented various options and alternatives, came up with a solution. Not wanting to put up more traffic lights, which would make it even harder for people to be where they needed to be when they needed to be there. But not wanting to alienate the "pedestrian" who in their mind promoted a healthy lifestyle through walking while at the same time cut down on air and noise pollution by not driving, decided to put a bunch of yellow flags in a bucket at each intersection that didn't have a stop light. This way, when people wanted to cross the street, they could take a flag and

wave it in the air so that approaching traffic would see them and bring their hi-bred state of the art electric run automobiles to a humming halt.

Two Days after installing the flags, a woman in a SUV on her cell phone, trying to make an aqua therapy appointment while changing CD's hit a bump in the road and spilled her caramel latté all over her expensive leather upholstery.

Glady Roseburg, an eighty-seven year old library clerk at the Braille institute was unfortunately that bump in the road. Yet now she more resembled a manhole cover with a little yellow flag sticking out of the top. Needless to say, the city counsel decided to rethink its plan, another meeting was in order.

As he snapped another fortune cookie, Calder was wondering why he had decided to actually meet with these guys. True, all four men at the table had grown frustrated with the behavior of the people in their community and their elected city officials. They were all anI'mate about wanting to do something about it, but what ever that was would have to wait for the next meeting, because this one was fizzling fast. Chaz and Harlan were now entrenched in a personal debate about what was more I'mportant "feng" or "shui." Although Isaac was trying to reel them back into his conversation about the bureaucracy that has shackled the shakers and movers of this once progressive East Bay city, it was no use. Between the banter of the two brothers, the clicking of chopsticks and slurping of soup Calder could barley make out a word that Isaac was saying. To add to the confusion, Isaac himself would become distracted every time this little pale waitress would walk bye. He would be ranting out some garble about city officials being blind to the needs of contemporary culture or this, that and the other when she would walk by or just cross the room to buss a table, and in mid-sentence Isaac would mumble out something to her in a really bad Chinese dialect, to which in return he received a look of utter confusion from the waitress. Isaac would then roll his eyes at Calder and exclaI'm

"She my Cantonese queen!"

"Really?" Said Calder. "what's her name?"

"I have no idea," replied Isaac with a chuckle as he jabbed his elbow into Calder's side

Just when Calder thought he couldn't take anymore of this conversation, Isaac's little "Cantonese queen" came over and placed a bowl of something in front of him that sort of resembled fish bones in noodles. Then she said something in Chinese that could have been a question or a statement; to which Isaac just smiled and nodded.

She then said something that seemed to I'mply "ok, if that's how you like it."

And she took a pinch of something from her tray that looked like little black rocks and sprinkled them over his food. Isaac's eyes followed her as she walked away, but Calder was eyeing the concoction in the bowl.

"What is that?" asked Calder.

Looking down into the bowl Isaac replied,

"I have no idea!"

With that said, Calder stood up and wiped his mouth and brushed a few cookie crumbs from his lap.

"Well, I need to get going, It's been a long day"

"We'll have to do this again," said Isaac glancing down at Chaz and Harlan who were now debating how to spell Feng shui, "when we're a little more focused" he added.

Calder left a ten spot on the table, said goodnight and headed out the door of the restaurant. The rain had stopped for the moment, and now in contrast to the loud noise of the restaurant, the street seemed peaceful. With a break in the weather Calder decided to hoof it the six blocks to his house. Although it was still cold and a bit windy, he couldn't resist walking through downtown Berkeley at night when the streets were wet.

Unlike San Francisco which lives to burn the midnight oil, Berkeley for the most part begins to slow down after 9:PM, especially during the work week. Calder loved walking through a city that hustled and bustled during the day, yet had the sense to quiet down at night and draw its curtains. To him, this was a sign that the gods were trying to keep a natural order of things. Making sure the city and its people, its anI'mals and energy, take their nightly rest.

Not only to rejuvenate for the next day, but to conserve its resources.

This was the type of energy that Calder was thinking about. Not the human energy created by large amounts of people living in the same proxI'mity with the buzz and peal of traffic that comes with a metropolitan community. Not the spiritual, metaphysical or biological energy that swirls in the atmosphere of a heavily populated city. Not the negative or positive yin and yang energy that pulls and pushes the thoughts and ideas of a congested culture that must learn how to live together.

"Isn't negative and positive the same as yin and ya...

"Paul! I am trying to write here" Maya snapped at him.

She hated it when he read over her shoulder.

"Sorry" Paul whispered as he turned to leave the room.

... The energy that Calder was thinking about was the sI'mple yet complex energy that comes from our natural resources. He was thinking Pacific Gas and Electric energy. That energy that seems to flow so effortlessly into our homes from pipes and wires at the mere flip of a switch, the energy that so many take for granted without really thinking about where it comes from.

As Calder made his way through the streets, he looked up at a ten-story building with all it's lights on. He knew that there couldn't possibly be someone in every one of those rooms working overtime. He knew there was not a janitor sweeping, mopping or waxing in every room either. Did every one of those lights really need to be on at ten PM? He started wondering just how much energy it must take to light up the city. Then he tried to guess how much energy it must take to support a society. With all the light bulbs, televisions, computers, CD players, video recorders, electric razors and digital clocks. And how about refrigerators, toasters, microwave ovens, electric stoves and blow dryers, and what about washers and dryers? Hell, washers and dryers use both electricity and gas at the same time!

"And don't get me started on Golf courses" Calder blurted out to himself, getting a strange look from a woman passing by.

A homeless man looking through a trashcan suddenly spun around but looked in no particular direction and shouted out...

"No, no, please, let's talk about golf courses!"

Calder was momentarily startled, but then gathered himself. Letting out a breath through his teeth, he looked at the man for a moment, wiped the side of his face with his palm and continued his walk towards home.

When he reached the porch of his building and started to fiddle with his keys he looked up and noticed the lights on in the apartment across the courtyard. He could just make out the top of someone's head through the window. He knew who it was, sort off... well, not really. It looked like she was stretching or some type of ll'mbering exercise. He was surprised that her lights were still on and even though her blinds were down, the shutters were still open.

Knowing that he would get an even better view once he was upstairs, he rushed to find the right key to the building before making his way up to his apartment. Opening the door to his place he reached for the light but then suddenly froze. He knew that with his apartment directly across from hers, that when his lights came on, they would I'mmediately draw her attention to his window. He stood there in the dark for a moment not sure what to do. As he looked out his window across the courtyard, over the redwood fence and driveway that separated their two buildings, he saw a silhouette moving slowly behind the gaps in the blinds. He couldn't tell if she was facing him or if it was her back, but she seemed to be in a robe or a dress and was drinking a beer or something, perhaps bottled water. He couldn't really tell what was going on with out staring. He tried to focus but realized that he was staring at a woman in her apartment from his dark living room and it made him feel uncomfortable. He felt like a peeping tom or some sort of voyeur. So even though it was hard not to stop, guilt gave way to his fascination, and he decided he had to turn on the light. But first he turned his back to the window and made sure he was moving around when he turned on the lights so that if she noticed, it looked like he had just walked in and was putting his stuff down. He went over and placed his keys on the counter, then picked up his mail and began leafing through the letters trying to focus on what they were, while at the same time trying to use his peripheral vision to tell if she had seen his lights come on from her place. He held a letter up to the light as if he was trying to determine what was inside and slowly peeked under the envelope to see what was going on across the courtyard. Her place was pitch black. She had either gone out or gone to bed. After a few moments of feeling foolish, he figured it was time for him to do the same. He had to be at work early the next morning.

As the main headhunter for the company "Head Hunters", Calder's job was to find people to fill specific positions in companies across the country. And since a lot of his leads were back east, he needed to start early on east coast time. So, after a quick shower he pulled a "Mrs. Smith's" chicken potpie out of the micro and settled into bed just in time to catch the last of Letterman's monologue on the late show. Sucking a piece of dough from his teeth with his tongue made him think about brushing but was too tired and rolled over to go to sleep. But as he lay there tying to fall asleep, he could not help but think about his neighbor across the courtyard on the other side of those blinds. The loud music she played sometimes; the chili pepper lights she put up a few weeks ago during Christmas. He then remembered one afternoon when her small bathroom window with its frosted glass was open just enough that he could see her through the opening. Well, actually all he could see was her back. She was wearing a bright blue shirt that had some type of embroidery on the back. It kind of looked like a golden dragon. As she brushed her teeth her shoulders shook and made the dragon seem to dance as it flickered in the morning light. He remembered that she was there for a really long time working on her choppers. At that thought, he slowly pulled himself from his bed and went to the bathroom and not only brushed, but even flossed before going back to get some sleep.

The next morning over coffee and corn flakes he looked up from the paper and noticed that the apartment across the courtyard had it's three big blinds pulled all the way up, exposing the entire living room and small kitchen to the world. It was the first time he could remember actually getting a good look at the place. The windows were wide open as if she were letting the place air out. He could see her dirty dishes on the counter and a robe, and some other clothes flopped over a red paisley print sofa. There was an empty beer bottle on the wooden coffee table in front of the sofa and another one on top of what looked like a big old black and white TV from the 60's. Calder couldn't help but wonder if she had drunk two beers last night or if it meant she'd had company.

Calder found himself feeling embarrassed for her. To have her personal life and lifestyle exposed to anyone who could see through the windows. He wondered if anyone else in his building could see her place as well. Could they have a better view from a different angle, or see something he couldn't? Did he really care? He suddenly felt curious and confused at the same time. Then he thought that she might be in another room and could appear at any moment, so he refocused himself and got his shit together then headed off to work.

He made his way through the damp grey streets to the Bart station. As usual, there was a group of kids from some elementary school going on a field trip and the teacher had no control. Kids were running all over the place while she was yelling across the station to another teacher trying use the automated ticket machine. Even though she was constantly calling out to the kids to,

"STAY IN ONE LINE!"

The children had now spread into three or four different lines and it seemed like every other kid was having trouble getting through the turn styles. Every five seconds this loud buzz would go off and a voice over a speaker would say,

"Please insert your ticket the other way."

Calder cut around two women yelling at each other, past a street musician and weaved his way through the chaos of kids and onto a train full of people reading the paper, drinking their lattes and talking on their cell phones. He managed to catch a quick glance of the San Francisco skyline just before the BART disappeared under the bay.

Although separated by one of the largest bays in the country, this massive body of water sl'mply fills in the indentation of land that connects San Francisco to its neighboring cities. But that connection of land sits on top of tectonic plates, which keep the relationship tenuous at best. The 1906 earthquake gave the peninsula a firsthand look at just how fragile that relationship can be. In '89, the Loma Prietta arched its back to 7.1 on the Richter scale. As these plates shift over the years, so do the geographical gaps between the cities. So just like a family that evolves through the years, there are times of strong unity and times of dissention. Times when the blood is thicker than the mud, yet times when they can't stand the sight of each other. It's this evolution that makes up the relationships among these city siblings by the bay:

San Francisco, the big sister, Oakland, the rebellious older brother, Berkeley, the young new thinker, and Marin, the lost youngster trying to find its way. And just like every other dysfunctional family, this relationship can be either envious or disdainful, united or strongly divided. And when a full moon cuts loose over the bay it can sway from incestuous to homicidal with the changing of the tides.

Although San Francisco spawned the summer of love, Berkeley became the city that Haight Asbury could only turn into a neighborhood. The pot heads and psychedelic counterculture of the 60's got too stoned to turn their momentum of the 70's into an actual evolution, and by the 80's they had completely forgotten how to smile on their bother and try to love one another. Instead, they were basking in their reflection from the disco mirror ball of the "Me Decade" and making sure that their hair looked perfect flapping in the wind from their BMW convertibles. They tried to speed away from an aids epidemic that despite it's devastation, could not stop the second coming of another sexual revolution in the 90's, where pot plants were replaced by I'mplants and the silicon valley was the space between a woman's breasts. As we rode into the year 2000, once again our so-called leaders were using war as an excuse to boost our economy and teaching us that they had learned nothing from history except that it repeats itself. And we hadn't even learned that.

As the new century began, the US was again waging war in a foreign country with no one sure why, California had another actor in office. And it seems that every single substance we know of on earth that we can eat, drink touch, smell, see or breathe causes some form of cancer. A disease we have yet to find a cure for along with aids and the common cold. We have also yet to find the fountain of youth, the city of Atlantis, Amelia Earhart, JI'mmy Hoffa, Osama Ben Laden or weapons of mass destruction in Iraq. We don't know how deep, deep space is or how deep is the deep blue sea. But thank goodness someone has invented a device that can count how many licks it takes to get to the center of a tootsie pop, so there has been some progress here!

7

Calder entered the office lobby after his congested ride on the BART.

"Good morning," chirped Phillip brightly as Calder walked in.

"Morning" replied Calder as he headed for his office.

"I'll be the only one in today so you can send me all the leads on the sheet."

"You got it sweaty," said Phillip without looking up from his computer. "I'll send them over in a sec."

"No rush," mumbled Calder as he strolled into his office.

Taking a protein drink from the small fridge in his office, Calder sat down at his desk. He turned on his computer and leaned back in his chair and waited for the thing to boot up.

Although the workspace these two men shared with four other people was on the fourteenth floor of a modern corporate building in the heart of the business district, it was by no means a punch the clock, hit the pavement, fill your quota, kind of company, and this was just fine with Calder. The system was working here. There were three offices with Calder holding down the one in the middle. The office on his right had two cubicles that were used by two people that only came in on Tuesdays and Thursdays. The other office on his left were Todd Miller and Jan Kenny's, and they only came in on Wednesdays or Fridays to drop off a contract or pick up a check. So, most of the time Calder and Phillip had the place to themselves.

"Head Hunters" was a company that was founded by Joshua Meyer. Joshua was a successful motivational speaker who preached the theme, "Success Without Stress." His winning concept was that one should set up the dominos for success, casually but confidently. Then flip the first one over, kick back and watch your work tumble into triumph. After appearances on "Oprah" and "Regis," followed buy a best seller, he was tumbling like casino dice all the way to the bank. He started "Head Hunters" prI'marily as a tax right off, but his dominos kept falling his way as the company landed big contracts. The rest as they say, is history. Joshua took the main office at first when he hired Todd and Jan to be his associates with Phillip as the receptionist. Then he took on Calder and the others to fill out his staff. It was in fact Calder who found the two others for Joshua.

Calder had grown up down south in Los Angeles. A town he now affectionately called the city of lost angels. And as anyone who ever grew up there can tell you, that at some point you will end up working in some way for the movie industry. In Calder's case, even though he studied some acting at Occidental college and even had some head-shots done to pursue TV work, but it was the other side of the camera where he found some success, as a film locations scout.

Since childhood, Calder had this knack of not only being aware of his surroundings, but noticing almost every detail around him; The contours of the land, the buildings, the people, the smell of things. He would notice strange cracks in the street, or the way a telephone pole tilted, or the architecture of a shop or the style of glass of a storefront window. He would play this game when he was in the car with his mother as she drove from place to place. In his game, he would lie down on the floor so he could only see the tops of buildings or houses or the sky. His Mother would ask him where they were, and somehow, he would always know. Now it was easy to tell by the tall buildings when they were downtown and he could smell the ocean when they were near the beach. But Calder would seem to know exactly where they were when they were downtown, and how many blocks they were from the beach as well as the direction they were going in. When they would drive through a tunnel, Calder would look at the color of the ceiling or for some missing tiles in a facade and he would know where they were. Even more Impressive, was his ability to always remember the details of a place even if he had only been there once a long time ago. When he was six, Calder flew back from Toronto with his folks after visiting his mother's family for Christmas. On the flight home they had a three-hour layover in Salt Lake City. A friend of his Father's picked them up at the airport and took them back to his ranch up in the hills for lunch, then brought them back for the final flight home. Seven years later, his family took a summer vacation trip to Utah and his father got lost trying to find his friend's ranch. But Calder remembered as a child that the airport was on their left when they started up into the hills, and the big rock that had reminded him of a battleship told him they were going the right way.

As they made there way down the two lane highway, the sun was beginning to set and his father was starting to get a bit nervous. Calder suddenly shouted out stop! He looked at a wooden gate set back in a dirt driveway and saw a rusted wagon wheel on the front of the gate and knew that the ranch they were looking for was right across the highway. His Father backed up turned the wheel and drove across the blacktop and onto a narrow dirt road. After about two minutes they saw the ranch!

"Amazing" said his father.

Calder just smiled. Calder would later use this skill of his to find just the right location a director was looking for. The director would tell Calder what he wanted in terms of ambiance, style or a certain era and Calder would find it. He had a great time driving all over the L.A. basin and through out the state and sometimes the country trying to find a location to shoot a film. He enjoyed looking through huge mansions as much as he did old warehouses. Breathtaking vistas and deserts were just as interesting to him as dirty back alleys and funky ghetto streets.

Unfortunately though, Calder had little patience for people and human behavior in general. Perhaps it was because he was an only child and never really had to share anything, or perhaps it was because he spent more time in his head thinking about things then in the real world, dealing with real people. In any case, he developed a low tolerance for a lot of things. And it wasn't long till he got tired of dictating directors, pushy producers and adolescent actors and decided to give up the job all together. Besides, driving all over town was getting old and the traffic was starting to get non-stop. The hours were so inconsistent that he never knew when he would get to eat or get to sleep. He was always tired and had no friends or love interest because he had no routine that he could count on.

So, he took a job in telemarketing where he had a regular job with regular hours. He had a small cubicle to himself and the only people he had to deal with were faceless voices on the other end of the phone. Now almost all telemarketing gigs pay on commission alone, but Calder lucked out and found one that paid an hourly rate as well. And since his last job left him no time to spend the money he was making, he had a good chunk of it still in the bank and felt no need to push real hard at work. This laid back, some might call "California Attitude" that Calder took towards his work turned out to be the hook he stumbled onto in the telemarketing business. Because he didn't seem to care if he made sales or not, there was no push in his selling technique, no phony plastic pitch that you get from some telephone jockey who could care less that you might be sitting down to dinner or sitting down on the toilet. Since Calder almost always started his calls with,

"Am I interrupting?", or "Do you have a moment"?

It felt like a polite conversation, and not a sales pitch at all. Consequently, Calder did very well. And coincidently, one day one of his calls was to a man who lived in the bay area named Joshua Meyer who so enjoyed the conversation that he told Calder to look him up if he was ever in the area. As fate, or luck would have it, Calder would move to Berkeley about a year later and do just that.

When he first started working for Joshua, Calder shared one of the four cubicles with Jan, but Joshua was in such demand on the speaking circuit that he could never come into the office on a regular basis. That was followed by the trend of working from your home, which meant no one showed up on a consistent basis at all. Soon Calder started finding Philip to be the only one at the office. In spite of the difference in their social and sexual preferences, Calder soon found out they shared the same cynical outlook on many of the same subjects, this led to many short but stI'mulating verbal exchanges.

Calder would be heading out for lunch and to be cordial, would ask Phillip,

"Can I get you something?"

"I'm afraid you don't have what I want" Phillip would reply.

"Thank God for that" Calder would say.

"Don't thank God, thank Barbara Striesand."

"She's married to James Brolin," Calder would say, as he headed for the door

"Oh, then I'll take one of each" Philip would yell as the door closed. And that's the way it went

Then, in one week a man with a smoky French accent called three times for Todd Miller. Calder started to tease Phillip about his behavior when he answered the phone, how Phillip would go lI'mp and spin his pen in the air when they spoke. How Phillip would draw out the conversation every time just to hear the man talk.

"Well, you've never heard his voice now, have you?" said Phillip.

"I don't need to hear his voice," replied Calder.

"Everyone needs to hear something that makes them feel good for whatever reason once in a while." Said Phillip.

"But Phillip," said Calder, "You seem to feel good all the damn time"

"Oh, I'm sorry," said Phillip sarcastically.

And that's that way it went.

Two days later the smoky Frenchman called again, and Phillip began spinning his pen. Calder was pouring himself some coffee when suddenly Phillip said,

"Maybe You'd like to talk to Calder, he might be able to help you out."

Calder looked at Phillip with wide eyes and waved his hands in front of his face mouthing the words, no, no, no!

"Well yes," Phillip said into the phone, "actually, he's right here."

Phillip held the phone up to Calder, who dropped his shoulders, and let out a big breath while rolling his eyes towards the ceiling and took the phone. Phillip made the sound of water on a hot skillet and touched his finger to in the air. "Tssss!"

Calder turned his back to Phillip

"Hello, yes...well, as Phillip told you Joshua is not here right now but... uh, uh, oh, really, well yea..."

Calder slowly sat down on the top of Phillip's desk. After a few minutes, Calder asked Phillip to transfer the call to his office. It turned out to be quite a conversation, when Calder emerged from his office Phillip was waiting.

"Well, what'd I tell you?" questioned Phillip.

"What do you mean?" said Calder

"Smokey voice, or what?"

"I have to admit," said Calder, "very smoky."

Paul LeRouque had met Todd Miller at a "Reggae on the River" concert in Northern California six months earlier and was interested in getting Joshua to come to Europe. But Todd had gone off to the "Burning Man" festival in Nevada, and had not touched base in two weeks. After leaving several messages on his cell phone, Calder decided to set up the contract with LeRouque himself.

When Calder booked the European tour for Joshua, he was rewarded with the big office and told to hold down the fort. In turn, Calder gave Phillip a piece of his take and even left a decent finders fee check on Todd's desk.

Landing the LeRouque contract seemed to give Calder a sense of motivation. And when Joshua returned from the tour, Calder had filled eleven more contracts with nine different companies. Now even though he had not had a run like that since, he was in good with Joshua; and he had basically and casually, run the show from then on.

As Calder settled into his desk, Phillip brought him the list. It had with about nine leads, but one look told Calder that only about three were strong possibilities.

So, after several hours on the phone to BaltI'more, Lancaster, Newport and Bristol it was time to get some lunch. Calder headed out to the lobby and found a sushi platter with all the amenities spread out on the sign-in table.

"Tada!" sang Phillip softly.

"What's this?" asked Calder

"Oh, I don't know," said Phillip, "It just felt like a sushi kind uh day!"

"Excellent perception on your part," said Calder as he sat down on the sofa mulling over the selection of raw fish. "What have you got here?"

"I got everything baby!" Replied Phillip. "Oh, you mean on the platter!" Calder rolled his eyes. "There's sashimi, California rolls, there's eel and some yellow tail..."

Calder began to put the fish onto his small paper plate as Phillip pulled a chair over.

"What's my share?" Asked Calder.

"Oh, don't be silly," said Phillip.

"No, no, what'd you pay for all this," Calder asked.

"Never you mind," ordered Phillip, "You can get the next one."

Calder stood up and headed back towards his office, as he called back to Phillip

"I know what we need with this stuff."

A moment later Calder came back with two bottles of Sapporo Draft.

"You can't have sushi without some good Japanese beer." said Calder

"Oh, you bad boy," said Phillip as he got up to lock the door; "I can't believe you have beer here in the office?"

"Oh really," said Calder somewhat suspiciously as he handed Phillip a bottle

"That's interesting because I could have sworn the last time, I looked in that fridge there were more then two bottles still in there."

"Really!?" replied Phillip sheepishly looking towards the ceiling. "Well," he continued, "I guess we should just be happy that there was enough today for each of us to have one with this wonderful lunch."

"I guess," said Calder with a sly smile, "cheers."

"Cheers." said Phillip

The two men clicked their bottles and didn't answer the phone for the next hour. And that's the way it went.

That night, Calder sat in bed and finished off the last two California rolls from lunch. Then, remembering that the last time he had eaten in bed, he woke up with tortilla chips in his armpit and ants all over the night table. He got up quickly from his bed, and threw away the cardboard tray and put his glass in the sink. He glanced out across the courtyard as he headed back to his bed.

Her place was pitch black.

He tried not to think about her, but ten minutes later he was up again brushing his teeth.

8

About a week later Calder found himself sitting in a booth at Purans. He had started with some soup and was browsing the menu while waiting for Isaac and the Zakorsky twins. The mood was somewhat easy until the three men entered the place and could be heard debating something or another as they made their way across the restaurant to the table. Isaac was in mid-sentence as the men sat down.

"I'm not saying it's irrelevant, it's just that we're there now and we should focus on how to get the hell out of there as apposed to this constant debate of how we got there in the first place. Hey Calder, how's it going?"

"Fine," said Calder, "how you guys doing?"

"No, no," said Harlan, ignoring Calder's question; "Getting out of Iraq won't solve one damn thing if we don't fully understand how we got into the mess in the first place."

Chaz was looking at the bowl in front of Calder.

"What'd you order?" asked Chaz.

"Soup," answered Calder as the waiter placed menus in front of the other three men.

"Not one damn thing?" questioned Isaac, "How about solving the problem of people getting blown up!"

"What are you two talking about?" asked Calder

"What's in there?" Asked Chaz, taking a closer look at Calder's soup.

"Um, chickpeas, mushrooms, ginger..." Calder answered quickly.

"Blown up!" spiked Harlan, "hell, people are gettin' blown up all over this world every day. And that won't stop till we stop making bombs."

"What are those green specs?" Continued Chaz waving his finger over Calder's Bowl.

"First, we must stop detonating bombs, then we can stop making them. Don't you think?" Asked Isaac looking at Calder for agreement.

"Looks like chervil," said Chaz nonchalantly.

"Mint and cilantro" replied Calder glancing from his bowl to Chaz and back to Isaac.

"Yea, well we certainly have created enough ways to kill a bunch of people at one time." Calder said to the group

"And shouldn't we first just *stop* killing a bunch of people at one time," said Isaac, "and then figure out *why* we are killing people in the first place?"

As Isaac was talking, Chaz reached over with his spoon and helped himself to Calder's soup, somewhat to Calder's dismay.

"You want me to order you some?" Asked Calder slightly annoyed.

"What for?" said Chaz bluntly. "I know how to talk!"

Calder looked at Harlan a little confused.

"No, uh...see, I don't like to share my..."

"Look," said Harlan, "When Chaz here decided to use PVC for his water heater and the damn seal burst from the heat and pressure, I told him right then and there standing in two feet of water," pointing a finger at Calder, "he should have used with galvanized pipes."

"Too damn spicy, "said Chaz wiping the broth from his beard.

"Yea, but did you replace the pipes first or did you start bailing water?" asked Isaac leaning in.

The waiter approached the table. "May I take your order gentlemen?"

"I'll have the lamb curry," answered Isaac, glancing up for a second.

"I headed straight for the hardware store," barked Harlan, "and got me some schedule 40..."

"It's burning' my lips," mumbled Chaz to Calder

"... plumbers grade galvanized..." continued Harlan

"And you sir?" the waiter asked Calder.

"But I kind of like it!" interrupted, Chaz licking his lips.

Calder looked up at the other men then back to the waiter. His head felt like it was on a swivel.

"Uh... I'll have the tandoori salmon." said Calder

"The salmon," echoed the waiter

"I'll try the soup" said Chaz

"... industrial strength pipe." finished Harlan

"Yea," said Isaac trying to prove his point, "but you couldn't put the pipe *in* until you took the water *out*. You could not solve the original cause of the problem," tapping his finger on the table to the rhythm of his voice, "without first dealing with the I'mmediate problem, correct?"

Isaac looked at the other men for agreement as Harlan went silent for the moment.

"And you sir" the waiter asked Harlan who was still staring at Isaac.

"I'll have the sweet and sour soup," answered Harlan without looking up at the waiter.

There was another moment of confused silence as the waiter and the other three men looked at Harlan.

"We're at an Indian restaurant Harlan," growled Isaac staring right back at him.

Harlan glanced up at the waiter for a moment, then he reached into his pocket and took out his glasses. Leaning forward he looked up and down the menu for a moment then tossed it back onto the table and returned to his frustration.

"I'll just have some water!" snorted Harlan.

"Regular, mineral or sparkling?" Asked the waiter.

Harlan just glared at the man!

After dinner and some spirited conversation about the state of affairs in the country the four men stepped out of the restaurant into the night air.

"Where are you parked?" asked Calder, as a woman approached the four men.

"Around the corner," replied Isaac.

"Can you spare some change?" Asked the woman.

"Uh, let's see what I have," Calder replied, reaching into his pocket. Finding a few coins, he handed them to the woman.

The four men continued heading down the street toward Isaac's car. Because it was still early in the evening, the streets still had people milling about, coming out of the movie theater, different restaurants, several bars and various shops which were still open for business.

"I remember in the old days when you could still see the stars here at night," remarked Harlan

A man shook a rattling plastic cup towards Isaac as they walked down the street

"Got an extra quarter? Pal."

"'Fraid not," said Isaac.

"Cigarette?" asked the man.

"Nope, sorry," replied Isaac.

"What are you sorry for?" said Harlan,

"It's not your fault. I don't know where these guys get off thinking that we owe them something or that it's even nice to support the homeless in this country."

Harlan continued as they rounded the corner. "It only perpetuates more homelessness. It's not fair that people like us to have to feel guilty for not giving some of our well-earned money to those who don't want to go out and earn it themselves."

"It's not quite that sI'mple Harlan and you know it," Isaac replied.

Finally, the four men approached Isaac's Peugeot. There were a couple of teenagers leaning against the car watching a couple of there friends doing tricks on their skateboards on the sidewalk. As Isaac started to open the door, the two boys stepped away from the car.

"Shotgun!" Shouted Chaz as he cut in front of Calder and reached for the front door.

"What! Are we in high school?" joked Calder.

"Ha, you're just mad cause I called shotgun first and beat you to the front seat," bragged Chaz.

Calder just rolled his eyes at Chaz, as one of the teenagers rolled slowly towards him on his skateboard.

"Got any spare change?"

Chaz looked at the young man straight in the eyes.

"There's no such thing as spare change sonny." barked Chaz.

One of the other boys mocked Chaz and giggled, "Sonny?"

But Chaz ignored the boy and continued.

"Saying spare change is like saying spare tire, it doesn't exist. It's an *extra* tire, not a spare. We keep in our cars in case we get a flat."

Chaz's voice began to clI'mb.

"And if I gave that *extra* tire away, I wouldn't have it when I needed it. Now would I? Chaz was on his soap box now.

"And if I gave away the extra change I have in my pocket, then I wouldn't have that either when I needed it. Would I?

So don't ask me for something that don't exist!" shouted Chaz.

With that said, finally Chaz clI'mbed into the car and shut the door, leaving the four young men to ponder his theory. Calder was more than happy to get out of the car once they arrived at his place. Even though the ride had been a short one, the confines of a small European car and the lack of conversation, except for Isaac asking for directions now and then, left Calder feeling congested and restricted. Sitting next to Harlan (who just looked out the car window) while he looked at the back of Chaz's head didn't help the ride either.

Once upstairs in his apartment, he clicked on his message machine and heard his dad's voice as he sat down on the sofa.

BEEEEP! The message started.

"Hey buddy, what's up" "I hope you're still planning to come down for my seventy-fifth birthday. I thought we could go to "Monty's" for steaks and a few beers"

Glancing out his window as he listened, Calder could see her through the half drawn blinds. She was washing dishes. There was a faint sound of music playing through her window, from the answering machine, his father's voice continued,

"Let me know what time you'll get here on Saturday cause I got an appointment at the VA, But you know how to get in if I'm not here."

"BEEEEP!" The message ended

"Saturday" thought Calder aloud.

Looking at the machine and then at the calendar, he realized that his father's birthday was next weekend. Calder pondered and searched his mind to think if he had made any plans. He then felt both relieved and depressed at the same time, because he realized that he rarely had any plans on any weekend. Glancing back out the window as he listened to his other messages, he saw that the dishes were now done and that all the lights were out at her place except for a small florescent bulb over the stove.

"BEEEEP!" The next message played.

"Hi Calder, it's Phillip, sorry to bug you at home sweetie but Joshua wants you to fax him the first five pages of Bourdain's book, as well as his bio and the press release. Joshua is leaving for Puerto Rico early in the morning and wants

some background information on Bourdain; for his keynote speech. Thanks."

BEEEEP!

There was a glow from the distant back room in her apartment...her bedroom door was slightly opened.

Calder thought to himself, "she was probably lying there watching TV or reading..."

After preparing the fax for Joshua, Calder sent it from his brand new "HP 1240". He then sat down to watch TV. He had purchased the machine and brought it home last month when Joshua went to Tokyo. Calder planned to take it back to the office, but Joshua told him to keep it at home and just buy another one for the office. Calder wondered if Joshua was slowly trying to get him working from home as well. He started channel surfing, slipping off his shoes, he put his feet up on the arm of the sofa and thought to himself out loud,

"That ain't gonna happen!"

Calder liked going to the office and having a workspace separate from his home. He liked working at a place where people were working. The fax machine was nice, but it wasn't a sign of things to come.

He sat there on the sofa and watched a show where a young Asian man was singing a popular sixties' soul hit in front of a panel of celebrity judges. The young man, unfortunately, could not hold a tune; and the judges were rolling their eyes and making comical faces, as the young man continued to croon. It was almost like the "Gong show" from the seventies but without the buzzer, or a Vaudeville show without the long cane used for pulling the bad performers off stage. Calder realized that the young man was only being allowed to continue singing so that the audience would be entertained by the judges responses. It wasn't about finding the next big singing star, it was about celebrities making fun of ordinary people and the TV audience was supposed to join in on the fun of the humiliation.

Calder clicked the remote to another station only to find an infomercial about a device that sliced, diced, chopped and puréed your entire dinner in about five seconds, yet the whole thing fit in the palm of your hand!

"No thanks" thought Calder, and changed the channel.

Now on the screen were two men dressed in full camouflage; in a boat matching their camouflage, fishing in the rain.

"Oh God," though Calder.

"Click,"

Now a muscle bound man with hair down to his waist sweating profusely to thumping disco music running in place on some type of weird workout machine screaming

"Pump it baby burn, burn, Pump it baby burn, burn, pump it baby bur...

" Click,"

A Mexican soap opera...

"Click,"

Korean news...

"Click,"

Wrestling...

"Click,"

"I had no money, no credit, no future, But at "Dave's Rent All World" they said, "NO PROBLEM!" "Click,"

The TV went black. Calder went to bed.

Andy Warhall once said, "everyone will be famous for fifteen minutes."

But I just don't think he meant everyone at the same time!

With over five hundred stations playing over 12,000 hours of programming twenty-four hours a day, nearly everyone in the world is on TV, being seen by the everyone in the world, doing everything anyone could ever possibly do, and never possibly do! There are so many shows on TV now that the celebrity status once achieved by staring in a TV show is hardly guaranteed. An actor can work ten years on a popular show, yet no one knows this person because the show is lost among the other two hundred shows airing at the same time. Sometimes you'll see a farewell special for a TV show that ran for many years, epitomizing America; changing the way the world viewed comedy, drama or whatever, and you'll say to yourself,

"I've never even heard of that fricken show!"

But everyone knows the dental assistant from Butler, Missouri who won on "Survivor." The once unknown dental assistant is now a guest on "prah" talking about her new book "How I Survived Survivor." Reality TV shows have elevated the ordinary and unknown plumbers, cops and CPAs, and turned them into household names. They take a super model, a *male stripper, an exchange student from India, and a homeless man living in a cardboard box, put them in a million dollar high rise condo in upper Manhattan to see how long it takes for them to sleep with, betray or kill each other and call it a reality show! There's the reality cop show that let us ride along with them when the CPA meets the CHP after one too many drinks, and we can watch the whole thing from the police helicopter camera. We all watched on our TVs from cameras in the sky when they cornered Rodney King and physically subdued subdued him. And we all watched from our homes as the police chased OJ's white Ford Bronco through the streets of Los Angeles. We can watch a war going on in a third world country, live, while eating dinner from the comfort and convenience of our sofa. We can literally watch anything at any time; ESPN sports network showing men's synchronized ice skating, then push a button and view the hunting of the cape buffalo in central Africa, or push the remote button again to watch prostate surgery in high definition! Another click of the remote and Martha Stewart is cooking clams on the Food Network. We can find out all about the life of the clam on the AnI'mal channel, and buy Martha's cookbook on the Shopping network. One can learn the history of books from the History channel. We can discover on the Discovery Channel, learn on the Learning Channel. There is The Western Channel, the Sci-Fi Channel, the*

Lifetime Network for women and Spike TV for men. The comedy Channel; the Cartoon Network; Court TV and the Outdoor Life Network, and they are all available at the click of the button.

There was a time when there were only about twelve channels to choose from. It would take about ten seconds to spin the knob around to find out what was on TV. Now, by the time you scan all the shows, the show you wanted to watch is over!

There is one show that shows us real accounts of things like lions attacking their trainer or someone falling from the sky when their parachute doesn't open, a police chase ending with a car full of drunken teenagers crashing into a wall. And of course, there is the video footage of a liquor store robbery that was recorded on hidden camera, with the gunman holding a pistol to the head of this poor clerk while screaming in his face. Ironically, this show is called "You Gotta See This!"

Uh, no, I don't think so.

9

Maya and Paul were finishing up the brick walkway they were building off the back porch. Paul found an ad for old used bricks in the Recycler. The bricks were free to anyone who would take them away. The ad said, "come and get em." So Paul went and got em! They had run the bricks from the house to the garage, going through the small garden that separated the two buildings. The garden was bordered by Irises, which now ran along the brick path. They had planted Callalillys in the back of the garden along the fence that also connected the house to the garage. Paul was on his hands and knees putting the last few bricks in place while Maya stood over him checking things out.

"Looking good, "she said eyeballing Paul

"You think so?" Paul replied?

"Yea, and the path ain't bad either!" laughed Maya, smiling slyly.

Paul leaned back on his heels, putting his arm around her leg, he spoke in a bad country twang,

"Wull thank ya dawlin."

Then he stood up and gave Maya a little kiss, and asked,

"It does look good, doesn't it?"

"Sure does." replied Maya.

Paul started to tap the rest of the decomposed granite down between the bricks with the back of his shovel.

"Wait a sec." said Maya, as she ran into the house.

Paul finished up as Eli and Parker played with the wheel barrel. Returning a moment later with a camera in her hand, Maya told the boys to stand next to their daddy. Paul was gathering his tools under the lemon tree right next to the new path and it was covered with new lemons. As Maya took a few pictures of Paul and the kids under the tree, she remarked how she was going to send the pictures to one of her high school pals back in Philadelphia just to tease her about the weather in California.

"I mean think about it," said Maya, "where else can you stand under a lemon tree that's in bloom and full of fruit in December"

"How about Florida" said Paul

"or...Texas, or Arizona. Probably even Neva..."

"OK Paul," snapped Maya, "you get my point, the rest of the country is shoveling snow and we have a lemon tree full of fricken lemons."

"We have fricken oranges too," said Eli pointing to the tree on the other side of the yard.

"And fricken oranges too," said Maya.

Paul had to agree as well, it was a beautiful day, with the new path now in place, the back yard looked great. He got the boys to help him put the tools away as Maya replaced some potted plants that they had moved to make room for the path. Paul grabbed two beers from the fridge in the garage and brought them out as the boys went into the house. He sat down next to Maya, who was doing a little weeding, and handed her a beer. Maya brushed her hands together to the dirt off her hands and leaned back against the tree. She took a long slow sip of her beer, then let out a long low burp.

"Mommy!" The two boys shouted from inside the house.

"That was your dad!" shouted Maya.

"No, it was yooooouu!!" the boys shouted back in full laughter.

"You're such a hozer," said Paul as as they both giggled.

Then some beer squirted out of Maya's nose, and they both burst out laughing.

"Thar, she blows!" spouted Paul.

Maya rolled over on her side laughing and trying not to choke at the same time.

"Ayeee maytee," said Maya tipping her beer to the air.

Paul stood up and started walking towards the garage.

"You know we're meeting my folks tonight for dinner?"

"Oh, shit that's right," said Maya.

"Who's gonna watch the boys?" asked Paul.

"Carrie said she'd baby sit when she gets off work?" said Maya.

"Oh that's right" said Paul, "Rollow's gonna pick her up at five and bring her here,"

"Well, if Rollow's here, Carrie-Anne will be doing more lap sitting then baby sitting," said Maya.

Paul mocked being shocked. Then speaking in a bad English accent, he held his beer in the palm of his hand and swirled it as if it were fine brandy and asked,

"Ahr you sug-jesting that ower doortur will be perfourming sum sort of lawp dawncing on her boyfriend instead of keeping ower childrin safe and seecuar?"

Well," said Maya. He's a very cute feller."

Paul leaned against the screen door and looked Maya,

"You think they started doing the "wild thang"?"

"No" said Maya," I think they've been doing the" wild thang" for some time now!

"Yea, I figured," said Paul. "It's just hard to Imagine."

"Well, you're not supposed to Imagine it!" said Maya.

"Shut up," said Paul. "You know what I mean."

"Yea, I know what you mean." I'm sure she thinks they're making love, but it's just sex. I just hope Carrie-Anne knows that. I think she does." said Maya.

"Yea?" questioned Paul

"Yea," said Maya "she's alright."

Paul knew Maya had her own ideas about sex and that they were a bit more defined then his. Sexual intercourse had three different forms of expression according to Maya. And she had explained her concept of the sexual trilogy to Paul more than once.

"Sex" was what people did when they first started having intercourse. It was guided by desire and physical attraction.

"Making love" is what people did who were in love, where passion, and commitment gave each person the ability to give all of themselves to their partner, emotionally and spiritually. It was where two people became one, where both were there completely for the other to enjoy the experience that could only happen between people who were truly in love.

"Fucking," well, that was a selfish act that was about getting off when a person was hot to trot. Not that that was a bad thing but fucking to Maya was about feeling horny and nasty and the need to release those juices.

Now both Paul and Maya had their share of "sex" before they met, with Maya definitely the veteran by that time. And when they finally got together, they both experienced "Great sex!" But it was when Maya actually "Fucked" Paul, that he realized he was falling in love with her. Whether that made sense or not in Maya's theory is still up for debate. But once they made love, the debate was over, and they'd been together ever since. Of course, this made total sense, and yet made no sense out of Maya's theory that only people who are "in love" can truly "make love" because Maya would admit that most people "make love" before they fall "in love." So, you figure it out!

The problem Maya was experiencing, was that not one of the three aspects of her sexual trilogy was being experienced, and she wasn't sure why. But her optI'mism perked up as she headed for the garage with her gloves and gardening tools and Paul blurted out...

" You know, I think I'm ready"

Maya stopped and turned with a sly smile on her face,

"Ready for what Paul?"

"Well," said Paul with a pregnant pause, "I think I'm ready to tell dad I wanna take over the business."

"Really?" questioned Maya.

"Well...Yea," said Paul,

"I think I'm ready."

Maya could not be happier. She had been waiting for Paul to figure out what he was going to do with his life. After college he had worked as a substitute teacher, baseball coach, landscape gardener and rec-reational director at the local park. But even though he had always had some type of job and was con-sistently bringing in some form of income, he never stuck with a job for more then two or three years. It had actually worked out well because Paul always quit working just before one of the children were born, so Maya had him as her mid wife, au-pair, and housekeeper right when she needed one. But during last year or so, Paul had been getting unemployment checks while trying to decide what to do. So, it was fair to say that he was on the verge of floundering.

So on the way to the restaurant, Maya decided to do a little strategizing.

"Well, I guess you could drive down to San Jose every day, which would be a bit of a commute, but I guess it could work that way."

"Or" said Paul, "we could think about selling our place here and moving down there"

Maya wasn't crazy about that idea, but she knew that if they sold their place, their mortgage would be a bit better on the outskirts of San Jose then what it was now in Berkeley, not that much better, but a bit better. And that could make a difference. Not that they were strapped for dinero, but if Carrie-Anne decided to actually go to college, they would definitely need to make financial adjustments. When they entered the restaurant, Maya noticed a stack of real estate magazines in the lobby and her mind started planning. She decided she would grab one on the way out. After they all they sat down and some wine was served, Paul's father cleared his throat.

"I have some wonderful news.

I've decided to sell my hardware business."

Now it was time for Maya's pregnant pause. But before she could exhale, Paul piped in,

"That's great dad!"

"Well, I think It's about time for us to settle down" said his dad, "I want to start that succulent farm down in Dessert Hot Springs I've always talked about, I think we could do it."

"And there are plenty of places for us to swing the clubs on the weekend," added Paul's stepmother.

"Well, that's just wonderful," replied Paul.

"Congratulations" said Maya.

The four of them clicked their glasses and the waiter brought the appetizers.

After a few more hugs and congratulations in the parking lot, Paul and Maya clI'mbed into the truck and headed for home.

"Well, I guess that settles that," said Paul.

"What do you mean that settles that?" snapped Maya. "Why didn't you say something?"

"What should I have said? Gee dad, I'm sorry but you can't retire now because I want to take over the hardware store?"

"Well, yes" said Maya, I mean no, I don't know what I mean. Couldn't you have suggested a deal or some sort of arrangement that would allow you to take over the business?"

"That would be asking him to compromise his plans," said Paul.

"And what about your plans?" said Maya, "You said this afternoon that you had decided to take over the business. You used the word "Decided" which I'mplies that you had thought about it, which means to me that you had some sort of plan in mind." Maya glared out the window

"Well, I didn't really have a plan, it was just an idea, and it didn't happen, it's no big deal." said Paul defensively.

"Oh really" said Maya, still looking out the window, "so one minute you're ready to take over the business and the next you're ready to roll over and forget about the whole damn thing?" Paul could here the frustration in her voice

"Look, you saw his face, he was happy, and even seemed relieved to be letting go of the whole thing. And that's fine with me, in fact I'm happy for him. So, let's let it go, something else will come our way."

"That's what you always say," countered Maya.

Paul fired back, finally raising his voice, "And it's always been true!" I've always found a job and things have always worked out, have they not?"

Maya pulled her leg up under her thigh and leaned in towards Paul,

"But Paul" she slowly whined.

"It will be alright," said Paul.

Maya sat there for a while in silence looking out the window feeling frustrated.

She finally asked,

"Where are they?

"C'mon Maya, you don't need... "

"Where are they Paul?" repeated Maya sternly.

"Under the seat," said Paul.

Maya reach under the seat and felt around for a moment and then pulled up a pack of cigarettes. She pushed in the truck's lighter, and put her feet on the dash board with her arms wrapped around her legs.

She took a puff of the cigarette; and stared out the window at the lights floating by.

"Can I have a drag?" asked Paul.

"Nope" said Maya, You're a drag!"

Returning home, Maya jingled her keys loudly and even coughed a few times before she opened the door, but still managed to catch Rollow and Carrie-Ann untangling themselves and quickly sitting up on the sofa.

"Hi guys," said Maya.

"Hi mom," said Carrie-Anne, straitening out her hair.

"Hi," said Rollow trying not to grin.

"Where are the boys?" asked Maya.

"They're down for the night, well except Parker, he's probably still playing Nintendo," replied Carrie Anne.

"How's it going Rollow," said Paul as he walked in the house.

"I'm coo." Rollow replied.

"I have cheesecake," said Maya holding up a doggie bag as she headed for the kitchen.

"Cheesecake!" said Carrie-Anne following Maya to the kitchen.

"You want a bite of Cheesecake Rollow?" Shouted Maya from the kitchen.

"No thanks I'm coo," Rollow answered.

Paul gave Rollow one of those looks and nodded towards the kitchen.

"Well, I guess a bite wouldn't hurt," said Rollow.

Paul nodded yes and gave him the thumbs u signal as Rollow headed for the kitchen.

Once the cheesecake was eaten, Carrie-Anne walked Rollow out to his car. Paul headed upstairs to settle down for the night. Maya was finishing up the dishes as Rollow's car pulled away. A moment later Carrie-Anne came back into the kitchen and put her arms around her mom from behind and kissed her on the back of her neck.

"Night, mom." Maya turned around and gave her a hug.

"Night, sweetie."

As Carrie-Anne started to head upstairs but Maya stopped her for a second with a question.

"Hey girl" Carrie-Anne turned around

Maya gave her that woman to woman look.

"Are you being safe?" asked Maya

"Safe?" questioned Carrie-Anne.

Then realizing what she meant, she looked at Maya with reassuring eyes.

"Yes, mom, I'm being safe. Don't worry. You've taught me well."

"Don't blame me," joked Maya as Carrie-Anne went upstairs.

On her way to bed Maya checked on the boys. She found Eli sound asleep and Parker heavy eyed in front of the TV playing "Super Mario Brothers."

"Time to shut down," said Maya.

"OK," said Parker.

Maya turned off the game as Parker slowly staggered towards the ladder up to his bunk. Maya came over, gave him a hug and helped him up into the bed.

"Night sweetie."

Parker crawled under the covers. Maya bent down to pull the covers over Eli, and have a look at her little man.

There's something about a child sleeping that always gives one a sense of peace, like a sleeping doe in the grass. She brushed his hair from his face and stroked the back of her fingers lightly against his cheek. His almond brown skin was like smooth chocolate and his long eye lashes were like shinny soft feathers that accented his perfect little round nose. He looked like an angel. Maya took a deep breath and headed for her bedroom. There she saw Paul lying in bed with his back to her looking at a magazine.

"Have you seen the channel changer," asked Paul with out looking up.

"It's gotta be here somewhere," mumbled Maya.

Paul started to look for the remote as Maya headed for her desk. She sat down in front of the computer and slipped off her shoes.

She took a deep breath and looked at the last thing she had written. She tried to get into it as she studied her latest paragraph, but she just wasn't *there. She just couldn't get her head into her work. She put her thumbs to her cheekbones and rubbed her fingers on her forehead. She thought about the first story she had written in college and how easy it was to write back then, how the words as they say, "floated off her finger-tips." She suddenly felt something under her bare foot and at first thought it was one of Eli's toys, but looking down she saw it was the remote. She bent down and picked it up.*

"There it is," said Paul, walking towards her with his hand out.

"I've been looking for that."

Maya started to hand it to Paul, but instead, pointed it at him and began pushing the buttons.

"Maybe this thing will turn you on!" said Maya

"You're such a horn dog!" said Paul as he grabbed the remote.

"And you are a fricken corn dog!" said Maya tightening her grip on the device.

Maya Williams
English 10A SJSU 1989

The End of Her Rope

Loretta knew there were no bad seeds, just the farmer who sows them. No one is "born to be bad," only bred to turn out that way. She knew that bad traits were instilled not inherited. She believed there was no such thing as "rotten to the core," it's the neglect of the apple that allows the inside to ferment. So when she saw her neighbor, Davis, bring home that little black pup, Loretta knew things could go either way.

He named the dog Lady, and at first, she acted just like one. Pretty yet reserved, friendly but cautious. She had these warm black eyes, which Loretta found comforting. This caught her off guard since she had always found black eyes to be cold and distant. Davis, her neighbor had eyes like that, black as coal and unemotional. He had sent those black eyes at Loretta, more than once across his yard. She could feel those black as coal, unemotional eyes watching her whenever she left for work in the morning.

Yet Lady's eyes seemed to release a sense of solace within their rich deep blackness. Loretta soon found out that Lady's black eyes could even sparkle. Lady's eyes would sparkle when she saw the kids coming to pick black berries that ran along the fence in the dirty alley that separated their two houses. When Loretta was hanging up the wash, she would see the pup across the alley tugging on that strip of twine Davis used to tie the dog to the porch. The twine dug deep into her neck, as she tried to get Loretta's attention. Lady's eyes also sparkled when Davis would come home from work late in the day.

Davis would walk right past her without so much as a "hi lady" or a pat on the head or a nod or gesture that says I see you there, I'm aware that you exist in this world.

Davis paid no attention as the dog pulled the twine stiff, begging him for attention while trying to bark and pant and whine between gasps for air. The dog would be choking on that thin twine cutting into her throat, only to watch the pair of size ten and a half shoes walk right by her without a word, without a touch. Leaving only the trailing sent of cooked chicken mixed with the smell of beer, tobacco and the hardware store Then the smack of the screen door as he disappeared into the house.

That's the thing about dogs, their memory is short and their commitment to hope never ending. That is why the call them "man's best friend," You can ignore dogs, neglect dogs and even beat dogs, yet their loyalty and devotion remains. In fact, it usually gets even stronger...usually.

Loretta would sit on her porch and watch this pattern of neglect going on across the alley. Davis would inevitably forget something in the car or have to go to the corner store for more beer or get something from the garage. And each time he would come outside, Lady was sure it was to pet her or play with her or god forbid feed her. As soon as Davis cleared the porch, lady was yipping and tugging that thin piece of twine, stretching every inch of her little body as he walked right on by on his way to the car. She would get quiet for a moment while he rustled around inside the car looking for whatever the hell he forgot to bring in. Lady, on her hind legs choking half to death with the twine tightly around her neck, her tail wagging in silence. Her black eyes completely focused on this man in the car. Lady was sure he was getting something for her. The instant he shut the car door and turned back towards the porch, the silence was again broken. Lady would yip and bark, as she bounced up and down on her hind legs like a kangaroo on cocaine.

Gagging and panting in an anxious fever for whatever he had in his hand. I'mpatiently waiting only to once again watch him walk right by completely oblivious to her desperate plea for attention.

Twenty minutes would go by before she would stop staring at that front door with those black eyes. Her ears up and head slightly cocked to one side in anticipation and curiosity, faithfully waiting for it to open. One hour later he might appear again on his way to the store. Once again, Lady gets excited, she is sure she can would go too. She stretched the twine and wagged her tail only to watch him walk right past her again. Lady watched him walk all the way down the street until he disappeared around the corner. She drops back down to all fours, but still stares at that corner for another two minutes.

A little later he would come around the corner with a bag under his arm and lady would be up again stretching that twine barking to her man " what cha bring me, what cha got for me." As he approaches she can hardly contain herself. Again he walks right by, her tail stops wagging as soon as the screen door slams shut.

On and on it goes, day and night. Davis goes to the garage, yip, yip, yip, Davis takes out the trash, yap, yap, yap. Screen door closes, tail stops wagging.

Loretta wondered why he even got the damn dog. She wondered how the fate of this innocent little dog could end up in the hands of someone like Davis. She also wondered why she even cared. Yet deep down inside, as well as on the surface, she knew exactly why.

Army brat was what they called military kids when she was growing up. And although she was no brat, Loretta was certainly army. Her father saw to that. Ever since she could remember she got up at six, made her bed and cleaned her room just the way daddy said. When he asked her a question, she answered yes sir and no sir just like Buffy and Jody on "Family Affair."

"Finish your breakfast."

"Yes sir."

"Get ready for school"

"Yes sir."

"Do we have a problem soldier?"

"No sir"
"I've been re-stationed, go pack your things."
"Yes sir."

One day when she asked her dad where she was born, he couldn't remember and had to dig up her birth certificate. Turns Loretta was born in Marysville, Ohio, where they lived until she was three. He was then stationed in Camden, New York for three months, then they moved again. They lived in Olivet, Michigan for six months then they moved again. Jacksonville, Florida moved again! Corpus Christi Texas, re-stationed; Crawford, Nebraska, Tucson, San Diego, move, move, move!

"You're a real trooper" her dad would say. "Your mother couldn't handle it. But you're a good little soldier, aren't you?"

"Yes sir"

Loretta remembers standing on the front porch of their bungalow. Standing next to her neatly packed box of "only the essentials" squinting into the sun until once again a big green army van pulled up, casting a dark shadow on her face and into her memories. As a little girl some memories were clearer than others.

A woman's figure under the covers at the end of the hall, a smooth back and a pair of sharp shoulders lying in a bed in the morning. That's about all Loretta ever saw of her mother. The subtle perfume, shinny black curls and long fingers, that's all she really remembers of the woman who "couldn't handle it." She died when Loretta was young and then when Loretta was twenty-six, she died again. Only this time for real.

Why didn't Daddy tell her the truth? Why was she surprised that he didn't? The only real surprise she ever got from her father was his attention, the encouraging word from out of the blue or small sign of affection. A pat on the head and a "hey there my little soldier." At least he new she existed in the world. Which was more then could be said for Lady.

Was it Jacksonville, Florida? or Jacksonville, Tennessee? They moved so often she couldn't remember. She did however remember Crescent City, Iowa, she was seventeen and it was the one town and one time they stayed in one place long enough for her to actually make friends. Yet the one friend she really cared about never stood a chance with daddy. Chris Coleman was nineteen and had his own place, strike one, he was opposed to the war in Vietnam, strike two, his mother was Cherokee, and his father was black, strike three you're out!

Loretta remembered the look on Chris' face when she told him her dad had been re-stationed, and they were leaving in four days. He looked like a sad puppy, a little sad black puppy with sparkling eyes.

Chris decided to have a going away party for her. All her friends cut class and met at his place. It was the first time she drank beer.

She had had alcohol before, but that was a sip of whiskey or scotch that her dad had given her at the officers' club and the taste was harsh and burned her throat. But beer was cold cool and foamy and went down easy, she liked beer. She was relaxed under Chris' arm and was having a pretty good time ... until she noticed the army jeep parked on his front lawn.

"Oh shit! She shouted, "my dad's here!"

Some how her father had found out about the party, and there he was in the living room shouting at her and smelling like the officer's club. He grabbed her wrist tightly; smacked her on the head with his hat as he dragged her across the living room to the front door as her shoes slid across the wooden floor. She never forgot forget the humiliation and the embarrassment. Tears ran down her face as he wildly drove back to base. Whatever feeling she had left in her heart for her father were left far behind in Jacksonville, or was it Jackson Hole?

When her father died, she received a package in the mail from the army. A gold box with a folded flag in it, and his army pistol lying on top with a few medals and a picture of his stone in Norfolk. One night when she came home drunk, she stumbled to the mantle, patted the box and said,

"How's my little soldier."

This became her little ritual, as did getting drunk, until one night she tapped the gold box and the pistol went off and blew a hole in the piano. She realized then that she had to stop drinking or take the bullets out of the gun, but neither ever happened. She came to enjoy the idea that she wasn't the only thing in the house that was loaded. She also wanted to leave her options open.

As the days painfully passed, it didn't take Lady long to realize that the thin piece of twine that held her in bondage was no match for her sharp little teeth.

After chewing through the twine, she spun around in circles chasing the piece still round her neck as it dangled behind her. She then dropped down on her front legs with her butt in the air and barked at the remaining piece still tied to the porch.

Loretta watched Lady play in the yard from her kitchen window. She popped the top on another beer, and as if on cue, a warm breeze swept through the dusty alley. The breeze took the blackberry blossoms across the puppy's yard. The wind had the piece of twine still tied to the house dancing in the air as Lady crouched down, trying to decide whether to hunt the twine or chase the floating blossoms above her head. As she crept low on her belly in the tall grass; her deep black eyes fixed on the flapping twine, her ears jutted straight up towards the crystal blue sky bringing in every sound and movement within her range. The angelic moment seemed to suspend Loretta in time. She almost went ll'mp. Her smooth hip bone which barely held up the 501's on her body, slipped out between the waistband and her short cropped tank top and came to rest against the cool porcelain tile of her kitchen counter as she watched the scene play out across the alley. The white blossoms in the red sunset floating above the black pup in the tall green grass reminded her of the short time and days spent in Olivet. The staff Sargent would drop her off at the range to wait for her father. She would sit on the sandbags doing her math, she would watch the bull rush blooms carried on the wind slip through the brown pines and green barracks on their way to some other place she longed to be. But just as the sudden shots from the range startled her moments then, the howling cry and scraping paws on the screen door brought her back to the present.

Lady had lost her interests in the twine and the floating flowers and she now begged for the atten-tion of Davis at his front door. Loretta knew what was coming.

"God damn it!" yelled Davis staggering out onto the porch with the sound of a TV sports caster slip-ping out with him

"What the hell," said Davis. and in one swift move he scooped up Lady by the scruff of her neck and took her back to the corner of the porch, where he dropped her to the ground along with the bulk of his his weight on top of the poor little dog. Davis pinned Lady down and retied her to the porch post. Pointing but not looking at the pup Stay he shouted, pointing his finger though never looking at the dog.

Despite the harsh treatment, Lady was on her feet and chasing Davis before he could take two steps for the front door. The twine went tight as a drum as she tried to catch him before the screen door closed. A sharp yelp as it tightened around her neck. The door slammed shut, her two black eyes staring in hope. Loretta rolled her eyes in disgust. She spit into the sink and rubbed her hip as she headed for the fridge, tossing the empty bottle into the trash.

Looking into the mirror it was obvious that beer and wine and the lack of carbs were making it very hard for Loretta's hips to keep the 501's up much longer. She had lost twelve pounds in six months and her clothes were fighting to stay on her body. Although Lady had not packed away the pounds either *(thanks to the inconsistent diet Davis provided)* the dog had managed to grow about six inches. Other then that, not much had changed and all the black berries were now gone. The green grass was higher, and Lady's twine had now been replaced by a rope. The only other change was the subtle disposition of the dog. Loretta noticed that Lady seemed less enthusiastic each time Davis came home. Her barking at the kids in the alley didn't have that come play with me sound to it anymore. It had more of a keep away, go away type of aggression to it. Lady was losing her patience with humans.

One late afternoon, Loretta was sitting on her porch finishing a smoke and beer. Lady was barking at the mailman like she always did. But lately she had started barking at him when he was still way down the street before he got to the house and would keep it up after he had dropped off the mail and moved on.

There was a time when the mailman would put the mail on the porch. Even though Davis had a beat-up mailbox on the street like everybody else, the mailman would come up to the porch to pet lady and some-times even leave her a treat. Loretta enjoyed watching the ritual and seeing the dog get some attention. But then one day, Lady chewed up some of the mail. Davis beat the shit out of her and told the mailman to leave his dog alone and to just put the fucking mail in the fucking box! After that, Lady still stood and wagged her tail when the mailman approached, but he stopped coming up to the porch and just left the mail in the box. So it wasn't long before Lady started barking at the mailman the same way she barked at the kids playing in the alley. Today Lady was showing the mailman that same disposition, loud and clear. On and on she barked even though the mailman was still three houses down.

"Shut up lady!" Davis yelled from the house, but she kept barking.

Yarp! Yarp!"

"Shut up," Davis yelled.

"Yarp! Yarp!" Lady continued.

"Shut the fuck up!" screamed Davis.

He burst out of the house full of anger and rage with a belt in one hand and a beer in the other. The kids in the alley froze in there tracks! Davis threw the beer at lady and then followed with the belt. The dog yelped in fear and tried to scatter under the porch as Davis kicked her. A couple of the younger kids started crying and ran down the alley. Loretta watched the dust and rope as Davis threw himself to the ground and tried to grab the dog out from under the porch. Loretta could hear Lady yelping and Davis cursing.

Loretta got up and went back into the house. She had seen this too many times before. But as she stepped into her house she heard a change in Lady's whining. The scared high-pitched cry of the dog became a low growl, then barking and snarling. Loretta leaned back out the door to see what was happening. Suddenly Davis let out a loud yell. The mailman stopped in the middle of the street. Davis pulled himself back up from under the porch. He was holding his forearm.

"You son of a bitch!" He screamed.

He looked around on the ground and picked up a rock and wildly threw it under the porch then headed back into the house. Loretta stepped out further to get a better look through the dust and tall grass. As the dust cleared, she saw the rope tied to the corner post. It ran down and disappeared into the blackness under the porch.

Two minutes later Davis came back outside with his hand bandaged. In his other hand was holding a baseball bat. He went straight for the rope and began dragging the dog out from under the porch. Once he pulled the dog clear of the porch, he began beating her with the bat.

Lady started yelping and fighting back, biting and scratching, but she was no match for a Davis. Loretta watched in horror as he pounded the dog repeatedly, "Bite me will you, you son of a bitch." In the alley, the kids were screaming and yelling as Davis raised the now blood tainted bat to strike the dog again when he noticed something out of the corner of his eye,. He looked looking up and saw Loretta coming across the alley towards him. She had her fathers pistol in her hand. Davis spun around and stumbled backwards and fell to the ground as Loretta raised the gun and cocked the hammer back.

Perhaps it was because Davis suddenly stopped beating her or perhaps she sl'mply had nothing left, but for some reason Lady didn't make a sound as Loretta came across the lawn. The dog barely even moved. The rope was slack, and Lady showed no fear or aggression as Loretta approached. in spite of the moment Loretta seemed unaggressive as well., her frustration was channeled and direct Loretta it created a smooth flow that contradicted her normal languid and wiry gait. It allowed a clean punctuation to the brutal act.

Two black eyes staring up at the one black eye of the gun barrel staring right back.

When the gun went off the birds scattered from the trees and the sound echoed through the sky.

"that's a good little soldier."

Maya had always liked that story. She had written it the first weekend she met Paul. She remembered how easily the words floated from her I'magination into an actual story. How she had sent the short story to "New Yorker" magazine. How she waited in antic-ipation for a response that never came. She sent the story two more times, but still no response. After her first book was published and successful, she sent a copy to "New Yorker" magazine, including a copy of her short story, but still no response. And no response was what she was getting now from her brain. No words were flowing from her brain and no words typed from her fingertips.

Writer's block had settled in for the winter.

It's interesting how the written word can be something that a person can get paid for to put down on paper. How a person's ideas and opinions can have value to so many people, that someone will pay them to write it down. That a good writer can become a millionaire by stirring up a whole range of emotions in so many people through their writing. Now there may be only a hand full of writers that reach that high a level of success. But there is still a large enough market that many writers can make a living just writing. While the rest of the world goes to work every day doing the common, ordinary jobs that keeps the world turning. A fiction writer spends his or her days writing down stories they make up in there head. Not a bad gig. Think about all the books on all the bookshelves lining all the walls of the houses in this country alone. Not to mention all the books in libraries and classrooms and bookstores, I ask, do we really need that many books? If so, there wouldn't be all those books in boxes in people's basements. How many trees did it take to make all those books? Does printing so many books have an Impact on cIl'mate change and global warming? I don't know. Maybe we should ask the lumber companies or the paper mill industry. They're the ones in power. On the other hand, "knowledge is power". We get knowledge from

books, books give us information, we thrive on information, that we get from books. Which is why we
have books on our bookshelves, and in boxes in our
basements.

But we also have magazines, another form of the
printed word. We have soooooooo many magazines.
Not to mention pamphlets and periodicals sitting in
baskets in our living rooms, dens, bathrooms, den-
tist office shelves; the glass table of the mechanics
waiting room; in the seat pocket of airplanes. There
are entire aisles dedicated to magazines in every
drugstore and grocery store across this country. There
are magazine choices for the desires of all people. Like
"People" magazine. We got "Us", "Time", "Newsweek",
"US News", "Motor Trend", "Popular Mechanics", "Auto
World". There must be a gazillion sports publications
along with food magazines and news papers cram-
ming all those shelves. High Times, Yoga Today, Yoga
Tomorrow. It just goes on and on. Do we really need
that much information? Is it really information? Or
just words on paper. Paper that was once a tree that
was helping control the cli'mate of this planet.

10

Maya sat at her computer wearing only her night shirt, the vinyl seat of her office chair sticking to her butt, her chin in her palm, staring at the screen, sipping cold coffee.

"Writers Block, huh"? Said Paul.

"Big time, I thought you were asleep" said Maya

"I was" said Paul, but I had this weird dream where we both were running down this road trying to catch this big rolling globe. We were like chasing the world but we couldn't catch it." said Paul. "

"Really? sounds familiar." said Maya.

"Yea", continued Paul, "and we were running really fast, I mean like track stars. But we were really straining to catch this globe, our veins were bulging, our hearts pounding in our chests, We were really stressed. We started chasing the globe up a hill, and the globe slowed as it reached the top of the hill and we started to catch up to the globe, but then it started rolling back down the hill towards us, and we had to start running away from it. It was barreling down on us like that scene from "Raiders of the Lost Ark". But instead instead of a big bolder, this was the world rolling down at us. It was gaining and gaining, and just as it caught up to us and was about to crush us, I woke up."

"Wow, pretty intense" said Maya

"Like you're trying to catch up to the world, while running from it at the same time. That's a lot of stress. We've both been there. We both know how that feels. Maybe that's why I can't write. Although I haven't been feeling really stressed lately.

Paul laid there in bed for a minute, watching Maya watch the blue screen. Getting up, Paul walked over and stood behind Maya, and started rubbing her shoulders.

"Oh God, that feels so good,"

She stretched her arms up towards the ceiling.

Paul knelt down and started to massage Maya's lower back. Maya slowly let her arms fall to her side. Paul put his arms around her waist and started rubbing her thighs. He then let his hands slide down between her legs.

"Paul? What are you doing?" asked Maya. Paul slowly turned Maya's chair around.

He gently pulled her legs apart, and then put his face in a place it hadn't been for quite some time.

After sharing some sweat, saliva and various body parts, they laid exhausted.

An elaborate glass chandelier that displayed the solar system hung from the ceiling above their bed. The glass stars, with it's soft light watched over the two as they slept. The next morning Paul quietly slipped out to take the boys to soccer practice, leaving Maya to her dreams.

11

C alder was staring at a zebra or maybe a gazelle, he couldn't quite tell. He was lying on his side, with his head on the end of the bed, and his face so close to his night table that all he could make out was the grain of the wood. The curves and contours looked like the face and stripes of a zebra, but when he squinted his eyes slightly the lines extended above the anI'mals head, making them look like horns and suddenly resembling some type antelope. Calder had always been a bit fascinated with how shapes and colors, within an object, could resemble something completely unrelated to the actual object being looked at He even remembered specific things from his childhood where this happened, like how he looked at his mailbox at a certain angle and it looked like a mechanical dog. Or the side of a bungalow at his elementary school, where the paint was chipped, faded and flaking, there seemed to be a whale breeching up to the roof.

After a few more seconds of playing with the grains of wood on his night table he returned to reality and glanced up at the clock. It was four am.

"That's about right," he thought to himself.

For whatever reason, every now and then, no matter what time he went to bed, Calder would wake up at around four o'clock in the morning and couldn't go back to sleep. He was used to it now, and so he sat up, rolled his head around, and stretched his neck. He clI'med out the bed and headed out towards the kitchen to make some coffee. Since it was around seven am in New York, he could probably make a few calls or at least send a fax. As he reached into the freezer for the coffee, he heard what sounded like keys or something metal clinking from the street below. Looking out his kitchen window he saw someone bending down under a tree in the shadow of the streetlight. They seemed to be touching their toes and stretching. *Probably someone lI'mbering up and getting ready for an early morning run,* thought Calder.

As he returned to the coffee, some kind of light reflected up from the tree. Looking down again, he saw that it was coming from a shiny pattern on the back of the person's shirt. It looked like an anI'mal, maybe a reptile or a dragon. Before he could get a better look, the jogger had crossed the street and disappeared into the darkness.

After another congested ride across the bay, Calder walked through the lobby of his building, on his way up to his office. He decided to stop at the newsstand and pick up a paper. He thought he might go to a movie that night and wanted to see what was playing. He had come to enjoy the comfort and solitude of sitting in the darkness of a movie theater with a big bag of popcorn and a cold drink, watching a good film. However, when he was younger and went to the movies with friends or on a rare date with someone, and he would see people sitting in the theater by themselves and thought it seemed lonely and pathetic. He felt sad for these people, because he had assumed that they no one to go with to see a movie. And yet now, he was the one scanning the paper and looking forward to doing the same thing, seeing a movie alone. Something he, as well as millions of other people did all the time. It made him realize how ignorant he had been. And in turn, it made him feel somewhat evolved and even mature. But at the same time, there was a feeling that may not have been pathetic, but was still lonely, and he knew it wasn't because he went to the movies by himself.

Opening the newspaper in the elevator, he found the movie section and took a look. There were a lot of options. There were the blockbusters and the independents, as well as the avant-garde foreign film scene. And from what the paper said, you couldn't lose not matter which movie you chose. This made his decision all the more difficult. By the time he got off the elevator he had become frustrated by the overwhelming choices of movies and his inability to choose which one to see.

"Morning Sweetie," said Phillip in his usual cheerful way.

"Morning," replied Calder, as he heading for his office. But then he stopped and turned to Phillip.

"Uh, look Phil, could you not call me sweetie, OK."

"Well, what should I call you, sour puss?" joked Phillip.

"How about Calder," he answered back.

"Oh, are we on a first name basis now?" said Phillip

"No,.. I mean yes, I mean, uh, it's just that if someone was here in the lobby they..."

"What?" replied Phillip as he sat up in his chair,

"you think they might think that your gay, or heaven forbid, that we're lovers?"

"No, that's not it. It's just that..."

"Sorry honey," chuckled Phillip, "you're not my type. Well, not really."

Calder stood there a minute trying to decide where to go with this conversation, but decided to just leave it alone and turned back towards his office.

"But if you ever decided to jump the fence, continued Phillip, "I bet I could show you a nice time,"

Calder swung around quickly

"Look Phillip..."

"Oh, I don't mean that kind of a nice time, although I've had no complaints." Phillip whispered slyly.

Calder took a long breath and started to walk away.

"What I meant," said Phillip, stopping him, "was that I could introduce you to some people you could probably relate to, people you have the same things in common with."

"No offence," said Calder, "but I find it a little hard to believe that I have the same things in common with," Calder made the quotation marks in the air with his fingers. "your people."

"They are not, 'my people'. said Phillip, making the same quotation marks in the air mocking Calder. They are just people, single working men, and women like you, trying to stay afloat in this world and make a living. They have fun, interesting lives and sI'milar interests as most people. They are intelligent people who enjoy stI'mulating conversation and having a good time."

"I'm sure they are, I mean I know they are. I am not naive. I grew up in west LA, OK." said Calder.

"Oh, well, I guess that makes you a homo expert!" said Phillip.

"No," said Calder trying to correct himself "that's not what I..."

"Well," interrupted Phillip, "even if you are an expert on homosexuals, which I seriously doubt. It's not relevant to the conversation anyway, because I am not talking about homosexuals, I am talking about people."

"Look Phillip, I appreciate your invitation, I just don't want to meet any people right now. I just want to find a good movie." said Calder.

"Well, there's a double feature at the "Triple X, said Phillip, "The boys from Boston and 'Ramrod Willie!'"

Calder just rolled his eyes, turned and walked towards his office.

"I'm just kidding," said Phillip. Laughing so hard that he started choking. He reached below his desk andpulled out a Sapporo from underneath and cleared his throat with a splash of beer.

When you look at the entertainment section in the paper these days, it seems abundantly clear there are no bad movies out there. In fact, every movie is not only good, but it's the best movie of the year or number one at the box office. It's the smash hit, must see, feel good, blockbuster, shoo-in for the "Oscar's" greatest performance ever!

According to the papers we should not even need a marquee, in front of the movie theater. We should be able to just walk in without knowing what's showing, because whatever is showing will be (according to the New York Times) "Incredibly entertaining." "A never seen before, once in a lifetime experience." According to The Washington Post. "Riveting Suspense", Time Magazine.

And each one has its own clal'm to fame. Oscar nominee, Cannes Film Festival winner, Critics Choice Award, A Golden Globe Award winner, People's Choice Award. It just goes on and on. Sometimes it feels like the publicity for films these days suggests that all we have to do is just walk down the hall at the multiplex and decide if we wanted to watch something "outrageously funny", "shockingly original" or an "electrifying drama" and whatever we choose, we know that it will be the best movie of the year!

According to the papers.

12

Calder opened the garage and pulled the tarp off the car. He slowly backed it out and put down the top. He rarely drove, yet when he did, it was always fun, because it felt like a new car and was always a little exciting. It also didn't hurt that he was driving a custom '67 Corvette. His father had always been into cars, and had bought this one brand spanking new off the show room floor in 1967. Calder remembers helping wash the thing every weekend as a boy. He loved rubbing over the bumper with wax and then wiping it off to find his reflection looking back at him in the shiny chrome. He helped keep that car looking good all through high school, so when his father was no longer able to drive, he gave the keys to Calder and told him to take good care of it, And Calder did just that. Its custom paint job was candy apple red with white metallic stripes on the hood and trunk. It had its original spoke rI'ms and chrome exhaust pipes on each side. It was a four speed with a 327 small block and its four-barrel carburetor made the motor purr like soft thunder as Calder rolled through the city on his way out of town.

Ironically, Calder was not really into cars, but this made him just the right person to drive a classic Corvette. He had virtually no ego, so he didn't care if he was noticed driving around town in a cool car. His vanity did not need a flashy red sports car to save a mid-life crisis that he wasn't having. So when he took out the 'Vette, he sat easy in the car. He never revved the engine or ripped down the street. In fact, he could not understand why someone would buy a muscle car or high-powered sports car in the city anyway. You see them speeding from one light to the next or driving everyone crazy on the freeway zipping in and out of traffic. Calder saw no point in drawing attention to himself, the car was really the show, and he let it have the stage.

As he made his way down 880, he hit the usual Saturday airport traffic, near the coliseum, but by the time he had passed San Leandro, things the roadway started to open up. Although Calder took it easy in the city, he enjoyed a little speed as much as the next guy. So when the highway cleared out, he let the Vette have some fun. He stepped on the gas, and pulled away from the small pack of cars he was in and found an open space with nothing in front of him. He looked over his left shoulder, a Jetta, no problem. On his right was a Saab turbo, that turbine might catch him in the long run, but it couldn't beat him to the space he was about to take.

Calder pressed his foot slightly on the gas pedal and that 350-stock block engine responded like a cat springing out of the bush and pouncing on the highway. Roaring out into the open, Calder shouted, as he petted the dash.

"Yea baby!"

The wind was whisking across the top of his head and he was moving along pretty well, when all of a sudden, a flash of bright red and yellow came out of nowhere and went zipping right past him. It was one of those Japanese racing bikes, and it was moving. Suddenly, another went by, then another. Calder looked in the rear-view mirror and saw a barrage of brightly colored bikes coming up fast from behind. As each bike passed one at a time, he noticed how streamed lined and sleek they looked, and how fucking fast they were going, some were almost a blurr. One of the riders slowed down on the passenger side of the 'Vette. The guy looked over at Calder. He checked out the car for a second and then nodded his head as if to say, "c'mon, let's go for it." Calder just smiled and waved him off. The rider hit the throttle and was gone.

There were now about six riders in front of Calder, and to his astonishment, some started showing off and doing these crazy stunts! One guy started weaving in and out of the broken stripes between the lanes. Another stood up on his foot pegs, and held his arms up in the air. one. One guy even put both legs over onto one side of the bike and started riding it sidesaddle! They couldn't have been more then 20 feet in front of Calder! Then the guy started dragging his foot along the ground! He must have had a steel plate on the bottom of his boot because sparks started flying off his foot like a welding torch. Calder's heart was pounding! He was scared to death, yet found himself feeling curiously excited at the same time. He wondered what he would do if one of these guys went down and a motorcycle and a body went slamming down on the highway in front of him. In all the excitement, Calder lost track of his own speed. He finally looked down at the speedometer and saw that he was doing eighty-five miles per hour! He thought about slowing down but saw more riders in his rearview mirror right on his bumper. They were drafting off of him. They were lying flat on top of their gas tanks and slip-steaming in his wake. He knew that if he suddenly slowed down, they would probably end up all over his trunk or in his lap. A red Kawasaki swung around and came right up next to him, on the driver's side. There was a woman on the back. But unlike most of the other riders who wore brightly colored racing leathers, these two were only in helmets, tank tops and shorts. They looked like the classic California motorcycle poster. The driver's helmet was red with yellow flames and his muscular arms displayed a variety of tattoos. The woman's tight braid was flapping like mad in the wind from under her solid chrome helmet that had an Oakland Raiders sticker on it. They both were tanned and well toned. The woman had tied her tank top in a knot under her perfectly made breasts so she could show off her six-pack abs. She looked at the car and pointed at Calder and gave him a "thumbs up" and an "OK" sign. Again, Calder smiled and waved. The driver then punched the gas and the front wheel lifted into the air. The woman almost fell off as her head snapped back. Calder gasped in shock! The driver held the wheelie right there next to Calder's door for what seemed like an eternity. He then hit the throttle and pulled away while still holding the wheelie. The girl put two fingers to her helmet where her mouth would be and blew Calder a kiss goodbye. She spanked the back of the bike like a horse's ass as if to say "gitty-up". And away they went with that braid still flapping in the wind.

As the bikes sped off, Calder slowed down a bit and let his heart do the same thing. Driving along, he let out a deep breath and then smiled. It had been a terribly frightening, but completely wonderful and exhilarating experience. Even though he had been scared to death for the rider's safety as well as his own, the rush of adrenalin during the whole experience was like riding a roller coaster that was out of control and the passengers didn't care. The idea of people who didn't seem to care about their lives and were living in the moment was overwhelmingly frightening, yet alluring to him at the same time. He thought it reckless and stupid, but gutsy and brash. He was envious of there behavior.

As he rolled into San Jose, Calder decided to check the traffic on the radio and was glad he did. An eigh-teen-wheeler had lost its payload all over 101 just south of town. and had traffic backed up for several miles. *What the hell* thought Calder, *I'll just slip over highway 17 through the mountains to Santa Cruz, then head south on highway 1 and then cut back to 101 by way of 185 through Salinas.* He also figured with the up and down curves on Highway 17, that this would be another chance to have some fun with the car. As he started his accent of 17 with Los Gatos behind him, he passed the Lexington reservoir, and to his surprise he saw a long red braid flapping in the wind about four cars in front of him. Maybe they had stopped for gas or something, but however it happened, he had caught up with them. Yet no sooner had he seen the braid and classic butt shot (that every girl gives when riding on the back of one those types of motorcycles) he heard the high whine of the engine and watched it pitch into a curve and disappear.

Not so fast my little ass, thought Calder, as he asked his own machine for some power, and again it responded. He started speeding up and moving through traffic. At first, he got close and even thought they saw him, but then they sped away. The second time he closed the gap by doing a nice inside move around another car and was close enough to see the logo on the back of her shorts. But then the bike made a slick move of its own. and they were gone again. Calder thought he had lost them, but he would come around a corner now and then and catch a glI'mpse of a helmet or braid and he knew they were still up there. As he was picking up speed, he happened to notice all the black skid marks on the cement barricade that divided the north and south lanes. He had never really noticed them before. As he came up to one curve, he saw skid marks in the road that ran for about two hundred feet, but didn't turn where the road did. The skid marks went straight into the face of the barricade, there were potholes of busted concrete and scarred cement with pieces of twisted metal sticking out. As he passed the broken wall, Calder eased off the gas pedal. He had seen his share of accidents on highway 17 before. The pass had a history of long waits in traffic because someone had broken down, or had a close encounter with the middle barricade. Calder decided to enjoy the drive instead of the view up ahead. Besides it was a beautiful winter day, the sun was out, the air was cool and brisk, but not very cold. From the top of the pass, he could see through the pines and redwoods all the way over Monterey bay to Carmel, it was gorgeous.

As he wound down off the pass, through Scotts Valley, he took the turn off south onto highway 1. He slipped past Capitola and then Aptos, with the mountains on his left and Monterey bay on his right. The highway changed from two lanes on each side to a wide open 4 or 5 lanes on each side as it passed Watsonville, then back to two lanes as it clI'mbed the long hill just before Salinas Road. He thought for a moment about turning left there and going back to 101 through Prundale, but he was hungry and had another plan in mind. A brussel sprout field popped up on his right just before he got to "Bunny luv" farms. He started looking for one of his favorite sights. Someone had started building a castle a few years earlier, and Calder was always interested in its progress when passing through the area. As he came upon it, he could see that it was now almost complete. It had two rook towers on each end and its renaissance flags were blowing in the wind. Although it looked a bit gaudy and made you think of a miniature golf course, Calder admired that someone with an unconventional vision continued building the castle. He pictured a type of modern-day Don Quixote, sitting inside, living out his dream.

The landmark twin smokestacks of the power plant at Moss Landing towered over Calder as he pulled up to "The Whole Enchilada". He stopped at the restaurant for some juevos rancheros and a margarita. After eating breakfast, he drove to another landmark in the area. A giant, two-story artichoke. He wanted to buy some for Rena. He also bought some deep-fried artichokes, artichoke chutney, marinated artichoke hearts and even some artichoke ice cream. Hey, he couldn't help himself. He was after all in Castroville, "The Artichoke Capital of the world!"

Pulling back onto highway 185, he headed towards Salinas, where he would catch the 101 South. The highway cut through large open fields full of, you guessed it, artichokes. They stretched as far as the eye could see. The ocean, in the far distance appeared cold blue and he saw the white caps jousting in the bay. The sprinklers were on in the fields, and with the sun shinning down it created millions of little rainbows, arcing over the wet thorns on the leaves of the bright green plants. Dusty dirt roads separated the fields and were lined with workers holding crates on the tops of their heads. The patches of sage and chaparral along the side of the highway helped to create a feeling Calder was having of being in a Steinbeck novel. In fact, anyone who has ever driven through the area would agree that the rustic beauty of the Salinas Valley had inspired the author's classic novels. Calder had always wanted to stop in Salinas and actually visit the "Steinbeck Museum," but he still had some ground to cover. So today, and once again he drove right through town and headed south towards Paso Robles.

The stretch of highway between Salinas and Paso Robles was a bit of a contrast to the first leg of Calder's trip. There was still the rustic beauty of the Salinas Valley, but as he made his way towards King city, the Santa Lucia Mountain Range now rose up in the west and separated central California from the Pacific Ocean, leaving the lush forests and breath taking cliffs of Big Sur to face the sea, while the vast fertile farmland of the interior to run east all the way to the Sierra Nevada's. Calder made his way south, passing farms and large fields along the way. He drove by the towns and small cities that sprouted up now and then along the highway. As he passed through Soledad, Calder glanced over at the MaxI'mum-Security prison that bore the same name. He thought of Robert F. Kennedy. Someone had told him once that Sirhan Sirhan was in there and whenever he passed by, he couldn't help but think about the man inside that had assassinated the young Senator and more then likely, future president. He was only a boy when it happened, but like everybody else who was alive at the time, it had become a dark memory he would live with for the rest of his life. As a boy, Calder just remembered the shock and pain, and the tears of his parents and of the people around him. Later as an adult, when he would reflect on what happened to us as a country, his feelings would be one of loss and sadness. He wondered how different things might have been had young Bobby become president. He hated how a bullet was still the great equalizer. He hated the message it sent to the world, and what it probably meant for the world. He started feeling a little depressed and realized he was getting too philosophical.

"Leave it to a long stretch of open highway to get me thinking to much," he said to himself.

He decided that some music was in order and he turned on the radio. The "Doobie Brothers" came blasting from the speakers, it made Calder wish he had a doobie to help him get through the drive. Thoughtruth be told, he hadn't smoked any pot in over two years and one puff would have knocked him out cold!

He was glad to be on 101 instead of Highway 5, which ran right through the heart of the San Joaquin Valley and for the most part resembled the bottom of the sea without the sea. 101 had its share of cute little towns and fun mountain curves with rolling green hills; that were dotted with ancient oak trees. And even though a lot of the oaks had died from a strange disease, they still stood like sentinels that broke up the horizon with interesting shapes and shadows in the small canyons and meadows.

The Salinas River flanked highway 101 all the way down to Paso Robles, popping up now and then beneath a bridge or an overpass to remind the road that it was still there. The River flowed all the way down into Lake Santa Margarita where its journey ended. From there the 101 had to fend for itself. It would spin through San Luis Obispo for a moment before taking a second to kiss the coast at Pismo beach. Then it continued south through wine country on its way past Santa Barbara before it died in LA, just like the oaks it had passed along the way.

A faded tan trailer sat on the edge of an olive grove just outside of Paso Robles. The sun was showing off an Indian sky as the clouds got ready for bed. A couple of cats sat on the porch as Calder pulled up to the trailer. The soft earth gave way to the weight of the car as it rolled to a stop. Rena was out front watering some potted plants. As soon as she saw the car, she knew who it was and turned off the hose.

"Hola Cho Cho," said Rena, as Calder stepped from the car, he gave her a kiss and a hug.

"Hola Rena," said Calder, handing her the bag.

"Artichokes! Oh, you remembered," she said in her slight Spanish accent with her warm smile.

"Your father, he is in the house, eez been waiteen for you." Rena told Calder.

"Thanks, you look great." said Calder.

"Gracias, su padre tambien, him never going to die!" said Rena

"I think that's true," said Calder as he entered the house.

His father, Eddie, was in front of the TV, watching football.

"Heeey yooou," said his father as he stood to greet Calder.

"Don't get up," said Calder.

"I ain't a cripple yet," his father protested.

"Happy Birthday," said Calder giving him a kiss and a big hug.

"Easy there, you almost broke my sacroiliac!" said his dad grabbing his back.

"Oh stop," said Calder, as both men laughed.

"Want a beer"? Asked Eddie, still lI'mping towards the fridge holding his back.

"That might cut the dust," said Calder, as he went over to the sofa to sit down.

Ever since Calder was a child, his father always joked around about Calder's strength when they hugged or shook hands. When they hugged his dad would grab his back and say something about his spine or his sacroiliac, and when they shook hands, his father would wince and drop to one knee and saying,

"Easy there cowboy!"

To this day, Calder still doesn't know what a sacroiliac is.

As he looked around he realized that there was something different in the room, but Calder wasn't sure what it was.

"Did you get rid of the plastic seat covers in here?"

"Yea," said Eddie, it was starting to feel like an old lady's house."

Walking back to the sofa, he handed Calder a beer.

"Sides," Eddie continued, Rena keeps it so damn clean in hear there's no need for em."

He sat down, and swung his feet up onto Calder's lap and leaned back on the arm of the sofa

"So, how's it going?"

"Fine, just fine," said Calder.

"And work"? Eddie asked.

"Work is Ok," he said, rubbing his dad's foot as he sipped his beer.

"How about you?"

"I'm OK," Eddie replied.

"How was the VA?" Calder asked.

"Crowded, as always." Said Eddie.

"What'd the doctor say?" asked Calder.

"He says I'm fine, but what does he know, hell, he's older I am. He listens to my heart, sticks his finger up my butt, and then we arm wrestle. If I win, he gives me the OK."

"Did you win?" Calder asked.

"Haven't lost yet!" said Eddie laughing proudly.

Rena came in the front door and headed for the kitchen, "Your son brought us some arti-chokes."

"Oh yea? Did you get me some of those deep fried frozen one's?" asked Eddie.

"You bet," said Calder.

"Oh good, Rena cooks them up just the way I like em." said his father smiling,

Calder glanced up at Rena,

"The fresh one's are for you," said Calder, as she put them away in the fridge.

"Gracias mijo."

"How's mom?" asked Calder looking back at his dad.

"She's fine," said Eddie. "I spoke to her yesterday, she said there selling about twenty-five pounds a day down there. They ship some of it around the world from their web site. She said she sent you a box of their new garlic and chive brie."

"Well, I haven't got it yet," said Calder "but I can't wait. They make pretty good stuff."

"I like that smoked Swiss, it goes good on a cracker." Eddie added.

"Well, I'm glad she's doing well," said Calder.

"She says hi, sends you, her love. You ever gonna get down there?" asked his dad.

"I don't know, I'd like to, why don't you?" said Calder, "Yea sure, as soon as I run a marathon!" laughed his dad, as Rena put the chokes in a bag.,"

Calder, sipped his beer and glanced at the TV, "Who's playing?"

"San Jose State and Boise, it's an exciting game" his dad then Eddie leaned back on the arm of the sofa and closed his eyes.

"Uh oh," said Rena suddenly, "there he goes."

Calder looked at Rena who was looking at his dad, who was now out cold." Well chicos, I'm out of here."

Rena headed for the door.

"You're not coming to dinner?" asked Calder.

"No mijo, I got my own mouths to feed."

Calder slipped out from under his father's feet and met Rena at the door with a kiss and a hug

"Have a good night, Rena."

"Hasta mañana," said Rena.

Calder watched her as she walked out to a three-wheeled bicycle sitting in the garden. She put the bag of artichokes in the basket on the back.

"Nice wheels," said Calder.

"Daz what keeps me in shepp, Daz why I will nayver die," she called back to him laughing.

Calder watched her as she peddled away before going back into the house. He sat down next to his dad and started watching the game.

"This guy's from SouthernCal and the boy can throw the ball," said his dad suddenly waking up.

"Well, that's what he's doing," said Calder.

, "Do you remember the score?"

"I think 27 to 14, but I'm not sure," replied his dad.

Both men watched the game for a few moments until Calder broke the silence.

"Did you smell ammonia?"

"No," said Eddie, but sometimes I don't."

"You want a drink of water?"

"No, this'll do," said his father, taking a sip of beer. "how long was I out?"

"Just a couple minutes."

"Did I miss a touchdown or anything?"

"No, I don't think so," said Calder, "but I was out side with Rena for a second."

"Then it's probably still 27 to 14."said Eddie.

That in fact was the final score, when the two men headed off to dinner. And even though it was a little cool outside, Eddie insisted that Calder leave the top down on the Corvette.

It was apparent that "Monty's" was at one time a "Denny's". It had that classic American diner look that on the outside screamed "Bob's Big Boy!" But the inside looked more like a roadhouse then a restaurant. They must have pulled up the linoleum and gotten rid of the booths, because now there were wooden floor boards and open seating. A bar that ran the length of the room and a strong Mexican influence in the place. There were sombreros on the wall next to cow horns and faded black and white photos of banditos posing with their guns and ammo. A couple of guys were playing pool, while Mariachi music came from the jukebox. Calder and Eddie sat down at a table in the middle of the room. An elderly woman in a traditional Mexican dress, looking more German than Mexican, approached the table and set down some chips and salsa.

"Hey there amigos. Something to drink?" The waitress mumbled as she handed them menus.

"I'll have a beer and a shot," said Eddie.

"I'll have a margarita," said Calder.

"You got it poncho," said the waitress as she turned away and headed for the bar.

Suddenly, the bird of irony flew in the window to point out that the waitress was in fact of German descent, and that the Norteña music coming from the juke box was dominated by the accordion, an instrument that came to Mexico by way of Bavarian Immigrants, who arrived in Mexico in the 16th century. Unfortunately, except for Calder, no one noticed, so el pájaro flew right back out the window.

The waitress brought the drinks and took their orders. Calder's dad threw back the shot of tequila and chased it with his beer. Letting out a breath of air as he wiped his mouth and leaned back in his chair.

"So, you got a girl now?"

"Nope," said Calder, but I'm looking."

As he laughed to himself at his accidental pun.

"Well, that's a start," said his dad. "Of course, getting a woman and making it last are two different monsters all together."

"Well, I guess you'd know," said Calder, not trying to be mean.

"Well, yes I would," said Eddie with a smile, letting Calder know he wasn't offended.

"But I wasn't trying to make it last anymore with your mother, you know that. It wasn't like we weren't in love anymore. We just weren't 'in life' anymore. We were going different ways and wanted to do different things.

You gotta' remember, we had been together since high school, and we really got married because you came along. By the time you were a teenager, all we knew was how to be parents, so by the time you grew up and moved on, we were ready to do the same, and we both knew it. That's why we are still good friends today."

Calder knew this to be true. In fact, Calder had to admit that his parent's separation was one of the most amicable transitions he had ever seen two people go through. They even socialized for a year or two after the separation, going to dinner and even to parties of old friends. They never actually divorced, and in reality became even better friends. It was Calder's mother that helped his dad when he moved to Bakersfield to live with his brother Stan who was dying of lung cancer. Two years later when Stan died, Calder's father opened a nursery in Rosedale California and would end up hiring a woman from New Zealand named Rosalie to run the place.

"Rosalie, from Rosedale?" asked Calder, are you kidding me!

Eddie would come to develop feelings for Rosalie, only to find out that Rosalie would come to develop feelings for another woman, and it turned out, that woman was Calder's mom, Emeline.

The two women had met on a Christmas trip that Calder's mother had made up to Bakersfield. After they first met, Rosalie had sent Emeline some plants she had seen in the nursery green house, but soon other things were blooming as well. Now whether Calder's mom was finally releasing some sexual desires she had kept suppressed for many years or it was that she was just discovering a new life-style, was anyone's guess. But after a few trips to LA, Rosalie settled the debate and Calder's dad was looking for a new manager to run the nursery.

Once again, the transition was as smooth as a silk purse. There was no emotional drama that needed to be dealt with and Calder's father took the whole thing in stride, saying, "I wasn't looking for a lover, just a companion." And he seemed truly happy that his ex-wife had found a companion that finally made her truly happy

In the next five years Emeline would move to New Zealand with Rosalie to start a goat farm and begin pro- ducing gourmet cheeses. Calder's father would sell the nursery and move to Paso Robles to retire. They were two people who at one time shared a life together, but now they are going in two different directions, figuratively and literally.

After finishing the steaks with rice and beans and beer, the boys were about burnt. The waitress had put a piece of birthday flan in front of Calder's dad and the kitchen staff was back at to work, after standing around their table singing 'Feliz Cumpleaños.'

Calder finished the last of his margarita. It was in one of those margarita glasses with a green stem that looked like a cactus. His father blew the candle out in the flan as the waitress showed up with the coffee.

"Damn I love this food," said Eddie.

"Yea," said Calder, "me too, but I think you're just spoiled by Rena's cooking."

"That may be true" replied his dad "but this food ain't at all like Rena's, believe me 'cause I know the difference. This food is damn good, but it can't touch Rena's cooking. They call this Mexican food, but its really Mexican American food, or "Tex-Mex" or whatever you want to call it. But this food is prepared the way Americans like Mexican food. It ain't the way they cook in Mexico. At this place, they serve refried beans, and you won't find any fish on the menu here except for the fish tacos, and they deep fry them and serve them in a taco shell." Eddie continued, "Now Rena, she makes black beans, with a little diced white onion and bits of green chiles in there, and she never refries them.

She also cooks these salmon enchiladas in this spicy adobo sauce that you would die for. Sometimes she even makes me this dish for breakfast on Sunday mornings called chee-la-kee-las, where she takes tortilla strips and melts cheese over them with this salsa verde and a little chorizo...man, they got nothing like that in here."

As full as Calder was, his Father's words were making his mouth water. A memory flashed him back to the fishing trips he would take with his dad down in Mexico. He remembered Veracruz, and the smell of fish and wet wood at the docks where they bought bait. He remembered the colors and the aroma at the open market in Guadalajara when they went fishing on Lake Chapala.

"Around here," Eddie kept going, "the only thing they serve at breakfast is Juevos Rancheros or a burrito with bacon and eggs in it, and...I smell ammonia," said his dad looking around.

"I'll get you some water," said Calder looking for the waitress.

He got up and headed for the bar, telling his dad,

"I'll be right back."

"Don't worry bout me," said his dad taking a sip of coffee.

Calder was still thinking about fishing in Mexico when the bartended handed him the glass of water. Turning around, he saw his dad across the room slumped over asleep in his chair. He realized that he felt somewhat spoiled by Rena as well.

When Calder's dad moved to Paso Robles and bought the trailer home he now lives in, he befriended one on the crew members who helped put the trailer in and hired him as a gardener and handy man. Palmo Navaro, was a third generation Mexican American who started out working for low wages in construction until he found the job at the contracting company putting in mobile homes. At first, Palmo was there every day, but after a while he only needed to come once or twice a week for upkeep and to do odds and ends. Calder's dad liked working in the garden as well, but Palmo said he felt weird getting paid for work when Calder's dad was helping him, but Eddie told him,

"I didn't hire you to work on my property, I hired you to help *me* work on my property."

Palmo had to admit he liked having someone to work with and talk to, and soon the two became good friends. Once, while Palmo was putting in a new faucet in the kitchen sink he suggested that his sister, who was already cleaning houses in Paso Robles, could come by with him once a week and do the laundry and vacuuming. Calder's dad liked the idea and Rena started the following weekend.

One day about a year later they were all working together in the garden when Calder's father passed out face down in the tomatoes! At first, they just thought it was the heat, but after it happened two more times that week, Palmo took him to the doctor. After a few weeks and a few tests, he was diagnosed with narcolepsy. Calder came down and visited and tried to help out. For some reason, Calder's father almost always thought he smelled ammonia just before he would pass out, but the doctors couldn't explain that one. Calder was trying to figure out what to do. He had decided to move his dad to the bay area, but his father didn't want to go.

"I just got the place together," said Eddie.

"I don't want to move."

Rena told Calder not to worry. She said she could come by every day to check up on him and that he would be fine. Calder reluctantly agreed and soon found Rena to be true to her word, and then some. Within a year, the woman went and got herself certified and became his father's full-time caregiver. She even rented a small place about a mile down the road so she could be close by. Calder could not help but feel a great deal of gratitude towards Rena, not just for taking care of his Father, but for making it possible for Calder to keep his own life as well.

Calder walked up to the table and pulled his dad's face out of the flan and wiped the custard from his cheeks. He sat down and looked at the bill as he finished his cafe ole. A woman walking by took a long look at Calder's dad with his head back and mouth wide open. Calder looked back at the lady with a shrug and a smile and said,

"It's been a long day"

A star freckled sky met the two men as the Corvette pulled out of 'Johnny's.

"That was a great meal," said his dad, "thanks."

"You're welcome," said Calder, "happy birthday."

Even with all the stars and a full moon, it still looked like a dark night to Calder who wasn't used to being out in the country. A layer of low lying fog didn't help the view in front of the car either as it rolled down the narrow black top with its tail lights disappearing into the darkness. There was a sent of pine trees mixed with the distant smell of cows as the 'Vette purred through the night.

"Boy," said his dad, "you sure got this thing running good."

"Yea, well I don't drive it that often," replied Calder, "So it's easy to keep her in shape."

"Well, she feels great," said Eddie, staring right at Calder.

Calder glanced at his dad and then did a double take.

"Don't even think about it," said Calder.

"I was just thinking out loud," said Eddie.

"Well don't think," said Calder

"I'm just saying," his father mumbled as he caressed the dashboard.

"Well just stop!" ordered Calder.

The two men sat in silence for a few moments as the car slipped through the dark night. Calder looked over at his dad who was still staring right at him. After another moment or two of silence Calder gave in and pulled the car over to the side of the road.

"Just don't kill us," he said, as he got out and walked around to the passenger side of the car.

"Hot damn," cried his dad as he clI'mbed over into the driver's seat.

Eddie revved the engine as he clipped his safety belt.

"Now take it easy," warned Calder.

"Don't you worry one bit young man," said Eddie, laughing out loud.

Gravel flew from the tires as the car fishtailed out of the dirt and back onto the road. Within a minute Eddie had the car doing sixty. Calder tried to relax.

"Easy there big boy," said Calder

"I'm OK," said Eddie, "this feels great!"

"Yea?" said Calder.

"Yea," repeated Eddie. "Remember what I used to do on riverside drive when you were a kid?"

"Yes, I do!" said Calder, "and you're not going to do it now!"

"You used to love it as a boy," said Eddie.

"Well, I'm not a boy anymore" pointed out Calder.

"Aw, c'mon," said his dad as he pressed on the accelerator, "it's straight as a bone for the next three miles after this turn coming up."

"No dad!" insisted Calder.

"What did I always tell you about curves," said Eddie.

"No dad!" repeated Calder.

"What'd I tell you," Eddie sang out.

"Find the apex!" whined Calder.

"Well, there it is," shouted his dad, as he hit the gas.

"Oh God noooo!" screamed Calder.

The car pitched down the bank of the curve and perfectly into the apex of the turn. His father then reached up and turned off the headlights. The place went completely black as Calder screamed out,

"Oooooooohh shiiiiiiiiiiiiiiiiiiiiiiiittt!!"

"Dad!" yelled Calder.

"Take it easy," said Eddie were almost there.

Calder couldn't see a thing. He dug his fingers into the seats as he pushed his legs into the floor of the car and pressed his back into the seat. A humongous head on collision flashed in his mind. He pictured a car full of kids coming the other way. He saw smashed metal and glass and bodies scattered across the road. He heard gravel smacking under the car as it started to bounce around.

"Daaaadd!" he cried out

"Just relax," said his father as he righted the vehicle.

Calder was wondering if he should grab the wheel or try to get his leg over to the brake somehow when he suddenly noticed how silent it was. All he could hear was the quite purr of the engine and the smooth spinning of tires on the asphalt. He looked at his father and something happened that seemed to transcend everything that was happening at that moment.

Eddie was looking down the road with this huge warm smile on his face. He was really enjoying himself and looked completely engulfed in the moment. His eyes were shinning like the stars behind his head and his fine grey hair was flowing through the cool night wind. He looked completely relaxed and at ease. The light of the moon reflected off his cheeks as he smiled at Calder, and even though they were going around eighty miles an hour, it felt like they were floating in slow motion. His father had this serene look of being content and at peace. It was almost angelic. Calder felt his mind start to relax and he let the muscles in his legs do the same thing as he unclenched the sides of his seat. Suddenly he started to enjoy this scary ride down a dark road in the middle of the night with the lights off. And for some reason, as he looked at his father's face, he didn't seem to care about the possibility of an accident, or death, or even life for that matter. He leaned back and put his hand on his dad's leg and continued his stare. His father took a deep breath and gently patted the top of Calder's hand.

"Pretty cool, huh?" said Eddie.

"Yea," said Calder, "pretty cool,"

"Kind of fun and scary at the same time," Eddie said.

"Yea," replied Calder

"But it feels good don't it," said Eddie

"Yea," said Calder, "it feels great, like we could do this forever."

There was silence for a moment...

"You want me to turn the lights back on?" asked his dad.

"Please!" begged Calder.

His Father laughed as he flipped on the headlights and the road came back to life. The white stripes flickered by beneath the car. Shadowed Oaks and chaparral peeked out of the darkness as they went by.

"I smell ammonia!" said his dad.

"Well pull ove..." started Calder.

"Just kidding," laughed his father.

Calder just shook his head and smiled. He then took a deep breath himself and leaned back and ran his fingers through his hair and gazed up at the dark California sky.

The next morning, Rena had sliced a few tortillas into thin strips and fried them in oil until they were crispy, then she set them on a paper towel to drain. She then scrambled some eggs in a wooden bowl and added some salsa verde to the eggs and scrambled them again in a cast iron skillet with some chorizo. She turned off the heat and added the fried tortillas strips to the pan and mixed them together and covered them with some Kojita and Asadero cheese. Then she poured more salsa over the whole thing and put in the oven for a few minutes until the cheese melted completely. She served this to the two men for breakfast with black beans and avocados along with "Agua Fresca" and coffee. Calder's mouth was still savoring the flavors of Rena's breakfast as he pulled the Corvette onto the highway, he had enjoyed his first taste of "Chilaquiles", and he wanted more as he headed north for home.

"Hi, folks, it's me once again Ralph Williams here at Ralph Williams Ford to tell you about some of the incredible deals you can get down here at Ralph Williams Ford in beautiful Orange County. You know, with summer right around the corner you should be thinking about a new convertible, and this one right here behind me is loaded and ready to go. It's got a 3.4-liter V6 turbo with custom rl'ms and leather interior. It comes with a 40-watt Alpine CD player with Satellite radio and state of the art 4-channel speakers with a sub woofer and I've got one in every color, make and model Imaginable with a full bumper to bumper warranty. And if you drag your fat butt down here right now you can drive this sweet puppy away for only 50 dollars$50 down, $50 dollars a month for fifty fricken years!

Our obsession with the automobile, which many call a passion, is nevertheless perverse. And like all perversions, is totally out of control. There are probably countries feeding their entire population on fewer grains of rice than we have cars. It's hard to Imagine that we have more cars than some countries have food, but then, some of the car lots you see today are bigger than some countries! Of course, this passion for the automobile has been fueled and fed to us by the auto industry from a very young age. Its seeds are planted via commercials and advertising as well as our parents and peers. It perpetuates within the infrastructure of our cultural, thanks to our dysfunctional nature to consume anything and everything in the path of our possessive behavior. But a culture that consumes everything is never satisfied with anything. And our fickle relationship with the automobile is a result of that unsatisfied personality. Which is why, this years hot Jag is next years cold junk. In fact, there are probably more cars in junkyards then there are on the road.

We have been conditioned to want, need, and must have, the newest, coolest, fastest and slickest set of wheels this side of that side and will sell the farm or our friends and family to get it! If aliens from outer space landed their ship on earth and saw our behavior over the automobile, they would probably wonder why we are so obsessed with a machine that pollutes the air while depleting our resource of fossil fuel and costs an arm and a leg to own and maintain. Of course, there are many people who sI'mply look at a car as a mode of transportation, a way to get them from one place to the next, a vehicle that has replaced the horse and evolved from our need to get somewhere faster and more efficiently. And it is true, the automobile as well as all motorized forms of transportation have allowed the evolution of the world to speed up, and in essence, made the planet smaller. Something many people might say is not such a good thing. There are countless cultures and civilizations before and since the era of the modern world that have evolved just fine without the aid of the automobile. Sometimes, the strong desire for something is only created because someone is telling you that you need it, must have it and are better off with it. But in the words of Charles Wright of the 'Watts 103rd Street Band', "Some people have everything that other people don't, but everything don't mean a thing if it ain't the thing you want!"

13

Calder rolled into town and was making his way through the city towards his neighborhood. He had enjoyed his drive home on the open highway, and it had been great to see his dad and Rena as well, but it felt good to be back in Berkeley. It was a fairly warm day in spite of the overcast skies; and street traffic was brisk, but not congested by any means. The coffee shops were busy as always as joggers ran up and down the street. As he came to a corner, Calder saw a man stepping off the curb and began to slow down. He waved for the man to cross, but the man waved back for Calder to keep going. Calder was already slowing down, so he again gestured for the man to cross the street. The man just shook his head no, and waved for Calder to pass, but the man kept walking out into the street as if he would cross just after Calder went by. Calder was almost at a complete stop now and knowing that the man had the right of way, he again waived the man across. The man flailed both his arms violently and screamed at Calder,

"Fucking go, goddamn it!...you're blocking up the street ass hole!"

The man came towards Calder's car as if he were going to kick it if Calder didn't drive on, so Calder gave it the gas but called out to the man,

"You've got the right of way!"

"Shut the fuck up and drive," the man shouted back.

"Jesus Christ!" Calder thought to himself, as he drove on, what the hell did I do?"

As he turned down the block to his house, he was still thinking about the man crossing the street. Like most people who drive, Calder had been screamed at before on the road, and flipped off on the freeway, but this he thought, was the first time he had ever experienced pedestrian rage!

He drove to the touch less car wash and had the 'Vette cleaned and washed, he even had it waxed and detailed. He took pride in taking good care of the car. After putting the cover on it, he closed the garage, got his mail from the box and headed upstairs to his apartment. He made a sandwich and sat down to go through this mail. Across the courtyard the blinds to her apartment were slightly opened and he could see the silhouette of someone moving back and forth. They seemed to be vacuuming or mopping and they didn't appear to be wearing much clothing. Which perked his interest even more. There were flashes of skin, bare shoulders and elbows. The sun light that cut through the blinds caught glimpses of long shiney legs that moved back and forth with the vacuum. But the vacuum looked a little strange. It seemed to have a weird handle that she had to hold with her whole arm. He thought he heard a Doors song coming through her open windows. He watched as the silhouette flowed around the room like a dancer, it was smooth and graceful. Yet the strange design of that weird vacuum handle made the dance jerky and clumsy whenever she tried to turn around to make another pass on the carpet. When she turned off the machine, the music got louder. It was "Ship of Fools" from Morrison Hotel. She headed to the window and started to mess with the blinds. If she opened them, he would see her face. But his blinds were already opened which meant that she would see his face as well. See his face staring out his window at her, possibly in her slinky tank top and underwear. He turned his stool around and focused on his sandwich and his mail. After washing his plate and glass he came out of the kitchen and saw that the blinds were now opened all the way, exposing an empty living room. The place looked neat and orderly. There was a painting of a geisha on one of the walls and what looked like various photos on another wall. There was a bookshelf sharing its collection of books with dried flowers in a ceramic vase. There was a poster of what looked like tomato varieties on the back wall of the kitchen. A calico cat slept on the arm of the paisley print sofa. Once again, he felt like he was snooping, so he turned on the TV and started watching a cooking show.

We're not allowed pets in this building he thought.
I wonder if she pays extra to have a cat?
Probably an extra cleaning fee or hefty deposit

He watched Jacques Pepin drizzle a beurre blanc sauce on a poached Dover sole and wondered if he could make it. He also wondered if he should be cleaning up his place as well. He went to the closet and got out his vacuum cleaner, one with a normal handle, and headed into the bedroom and started on the carpet.

Later that night at "The Fisherman's Grotto," Carder found himself leaning over a bowl of bouillabaisse trying to explain his experience on the street to Isaac and the Zakorsky brothers.

"I mean, he had the right of way," Calder pointed out, with the scent of Shellfish and saffron floating up from his bowl.

"Yea, well that's America for you", said Isaac, responding to the story

"You try to be polite, and people act like your patronizing them, you go about your business and you're a rude son of a bitch! You can't win."

"America, shmerica", said Harlan. "Don't go painting the whole country on the same crazy canvas we have here in California. There are plenty of places that follow the rules of the nature of society. People in New York wouldn't step off a curb in front of a car, they know their ass would be grass!"

"Well, actually pavement", chuckled Chaz as he slurped on some clam chowder.

"Very funny," replied Isaac as a waiter set a plate down in front of him.

"What'd you order?" asked Chaz looking curiously at Isaac's food as bits of chowder trickled down his beard.

"You take on the traffic back east," continued Harlan, and you'll get your butt run over! But out here, people don't follow their true Impulses. They're too wimpy to act out what they're really feeling."

"Do you know how many people are in jail because they acted on their Impulses?" pointed out Calder.

"Do you know how many people are dead," said Isaac, "because people acted out on," he stopped in mid-sentence and glanced up at Chaz, who was still staring at his plate...

"It's Skate." explained Isaac

Chaz gave Isaac the same strange look he was giving the plate of fish. Calder noticed the pieces of clams and potatoes stuck in Chaz's beard.

"It's the fins of a sting ray," explained Isaac. "They sauté it in butter and garlic."

"Why don't they just call it that?" asked Chaz, biting down on a piece of French bread.

"You know," said Harlan. Me and Chaz were sittin in the truck the other day at a stoplight, with it's politically correct beep tones for the deaf, and it's left turn arrows and crossing lights with it's little lit numbers countin down so that everyone knows exactly when the lights going to change." Harlan started counting down out loud, "Five, four, three, two, hell when the lights red you stop, when it's green you walk across the damn street"

"Makes sense to me" said Chaz, crusts of bread trickled down his face and joined the bits of chowder on his chin.

"So, the lights about to change" said Harlan.

"It's already yellow!" added Chaz.

Calder was half way listening to Harlan and half way distracted by the clams and crumbs gathering in Chaz's beard.

"When these three little snots", snorts Harlan, "start walking across the street. Now you'd think they'd start runnin or at least joggin' a bit or something, I mean the lights already yellow."

You got some shmootz on your chin," said Calder waiving his hand in the air to Chaz.

"But nooooo," continues Harlan, "they just sashayed out in front of all these cars with their pants hanging down as low as can be, just staring at all the drivers waiting for them to cross, just daring someone to honk a horn or god forbid try to drive forward, even though all the cars have got the green light by now."

Calder was trying to pay attention, but he couldn't help wanting Chaz to wipe his beard. It was like when someone is talking to you, but they have a little booger sticking out of their nose or a strange mole on their face, you just can't focus on what they're saying.

"Someone tries that in Brooklyn, they would be road kill", said Harlan.

"That's right", agreed Chaz.

"And Brooklyn ain't the only place where people know whose got the right of way between the curbs," stated Harlan.

"Well actually," said Isaac, "Pedestrians have the right of way even in the street."

"They have the right of way everywhere", said Calder.

"Now wait a second", said Harlan. If I drive up onto the sidewalk and run somebody over, I go to jail, that's fine. But if someone runs onto the freeway and I run them over, they're not gonna put me in jail."

"No," said Isaac. "They wouldn't put you in jail, But that person would still have the right of way. And you would be expected to try to stop."

"No", said Harlan, "They wouldn't expect me to try to stop, and they wouldn't put me in jail because that person is an idiot. And I would be an idiot if I tried to stop a car at seventy miles an hour because some other idiot ran out on the highway!"

"But by law", said Calder, not believing he was getting into this conversation, "You would have to at least try to stop, because that person would still have the right of way."

"Well actually", again said Isaac. "Pedestrians aren't allowed on the freeway."

"That's not the point here", said Calder flexing his finger in the air as he glared at Isaac.

"Well, I wouldn't try to stop." said Chaz.

"Me niether," echoed Harlan

"How could you not try to stop", said Isaac. "You couldn't help yourself. Your reflexes would take over, you'd... try to hit the brakes or swerve or something."

"What?" said Harlan, "and go into a skid at seventy miles an hour?"

"Or swerve into a car next to you or slam into the rail!" said Chaz, "Not me."

Harlan leaned into the table and pointed a fork at Calder, and spouted,

"If some fool runs onto the railroad tracks, does the train conductor try to hit the brakes? Nope, he's not going to jeopardize all the other people on the train just for one idiot on the tracks."

"I think you're getting off the track, and missing the point here," said Calder

"C'mon," said Isaac. There's a big difference between stopping a car at seventy miles an hour and stopping a train at seventy miles an hour. Even you know that, Harlan.

"It's all relative," replied Harlan. Waving off Isaac.

"No it's not," said Isaac, raising his voice. "A train weighs fifty fucking tons!"

"Well, a car has brakes to make it stop" chirped Harlan "And a train has brakes to make it stop, so like I said, it's all relative".

"I think a train weighs more then 50 tons," mumbled Chaz.

"This conversation is getting ridiculous," said Calder.

"What do you mean "even I know that" said Harlan, looking at Isaac.

There was a second of uncomfortable silence, as Issac looked back at Harlan

"What I meant was..." started Issac

"You calling me ignorant?" asked Harlan.

Isaac let out a deep breath and rubbed the side of his face, "No Harlan" Said Issac...what I meant was..."

Calder interrupted, "Look it's getting late, and I need to get out of here."

"I think it's more like 200 or 300 hundred tons," said Chaz

"Shut up Chaz" said Harlan still staring at Isaac.

"Look, you missed my point," said Isaac.

"And you missing my point!" said Harlan

"What is your point," asked Calder in frustration.

"My point," Mr. Smarty Pants, said Harlan, giving Calder a sharp stare before looking back at Isaac. Is that if I were behind the wheel, instead of my brother, those little law breaking niggers would have tasted my tires."

Calder was momentarily shocked. Isaac furrowed his brow and leaned back in his chair. Both men were now looking right at Harlan.

"What!" said Harlan... "Oh, I see, they can call each other nigger but I can't call them nigger."

"It's not that you can't," said Calder. It's that you shouldn't, it's a derogatory term.

"A derogatory term" mocked Chaz

"It's offensive," said Isaac.

"Well, they don't seem to be offended when they call each other nigger," said Harlan.

People were starting to look at their table now.

"You think you could lower your voice a bit?" asked Calder.

"Look," said Harlan. "You think just maybe they heard the damn word so much and used it so much that it now has a different meaning to them. Maybe you boys are too young to remember Lenny Bruce," touted Harlan.

"Who?" Asked Isaac.

"No, I've heard of Lenny Bruce," Calder reluctantly admitted.

Calder suddenly found himself in the frustrating position of knowing Harlan was about to make a valid point that he himself agreed with, but it supported Harlan's invalid use of a word, which he disagreed with.

"Lenny Bruce," said Calder, explaining to Isaac. "Was a popular yet controversial comedian during the 60's, and one time he opened one of his shows with a monologue where he looked out into the audience and seemed to be pointing out what a great crowd they had that night. But then he started saying, Look, there's a nigger over there, and there's a spick over there and a wop over here and a chink right there he started using all the classic racial slurs to describe the people in the audience. He went on and on, no one was spared. The audience started to get offended and agitated and upset. But at the end of his monologue, he pointed out that if everyone used these racial slurs over and over again, that eventually they wouldn't mean a thing anymore. And never again would a little black child come home crying because someone called them a nigger."

"Interesting," said Isaac.

"Thinking about the theory, I've never thought about it that way."

"Who's the ignorant one now?" said Harlan.

"Look," said Isaac. "I wasn't calling you...

Calder interrupting Isaac, stood up in frustration, and said,

"I got to go." He tossed his napkin down on the table in front of Chaz, "Wipe your mouth."

Chaz looked up, acting insulted as Calder walked away, then glanced around the table, "What's his problem?"

Harlan was still staring straight at Isaac

"What's *your* problem?"

After leaving the Grotto, Calder decided to head down 4th Street to get a muffin from the Ocean View Bakery for tomorrow's breakfast. As he walked down the street, he noticed a group of people sitting at a table having drinks. They were on the patio of a sidewalk café. He suddenly realized that he knew one of the people at the table. It was Phillip. He was talking loudly, and they were all laughing.

At first, he thought about crossing the street, but for some reason he didn't. He thought maybe he could walk by without being noticed. No such luck.

"Hey sweety" Phillip called out to him.

The faces of several strangers looked at him, as Phillip got up and walked towards Calder.

"Hey Phillip," said Calder, trying not to slow down.

"What are you doing here around here?" Asked Phillip.

"I live around here, just getting a muffin" replied Calder, pointing towards the bakery.

Realizing it would be rude if he kept walking, he stopped as Phillip approached,

"What brings you to the East Bay?" Calder asked

"I just came to meet some of my friends," said Phillip, "come over and say hi."

"Oh, uh, no, I'm just..."

"Oh, come on," Pleaded Phillip, "you're not gonna diss me in front of my friends are you?"

"Well, No, I wouldn't do that. Replied Calder, "Its just that I don't want to interrupt you and your..."

"Oh don't be silly, come over here and let me buy you a drink" said Phillip, grabbing Calder by the arm and walking towards the table.

Calder walked up to the group and stood next the table.

Pointing to his friends, Phillip introduced everyone,

"Calder this is Robert, Kayla and Cho Cho, everyone this is Calder"

"Hi," said Cho Cho

"Nice to meet you," said Robert

Phillip grabbed another chair from an empty table, as Kayla spoke to Calder,

"Hi. "So, you're Phillip's boss, where he works, is that right?"

"Well, I wouldn't say that," said Calder.

"I just run the office. In fact, Phillip really is the one who runs the place. I just chase down leads for the owner of the company." Calder said.

"Oh your just being modest," said Phillip putting a chair down behind Calder, "Joshua leaves for months at a time leaving you in charge."

"You want something to drink?" Asked Cho Cho, as Calder sat down

"Uh, ok, sure, why not," replied Calder.

Cho Cho was obviously gay, thought Calder. Watching the man waive wave his fingers in the air trying to get the waiter's attention. The way he fluttered his fingers in the air at the waiter and then pointed at everyone's drink, spinning these circles over the table, and then gesturing the waiter over. It was all so flowing, and feminine.

Kayla herself was the typical classic lesbian, as far as Calder could tell. She had a short cropped, almost buzz hair cut with an orange stripe running down the side. There were various piercings in her ear, lip and nose and she was wearing black painter pants and a red and white striped Dickey's work shirt. He was still trying to size up Robert, as the waiter approached the table and looked at Cho Cho.

"Ready for another?" the waiter asked.

"I would love another Mai Tai." Said Cho Cho. "And this guy needs a drink." Pointing to Calder.

"What would you like?" Asked the waiter.

"You got Saporro?" Calder asked.

"Sure do," the waiter replied.

"That sounds good." Said Calder

"And how's that apple Martini?" The waiter asked Phillip.

"I'm not sure," answered Phillip. "I think I should try another one before I decide." He said sheepishly.

"You got it," said the waiter, who then turned to Kayla, "Another Mojito as well?"

"Why not?" Replied Kayla.

"And another Bud for you," he said pointing his pencil at Robert.

"No, no". Said Robert. "I'm Fine".

Well, he's obviously straight, thought Calder.

As the conversations progressed, Calder found out that Kayla worked as a personal secretary for a woman who wrote children's books, Cho Cho was a 911 operator and Robert worked for an insurance company.

"And what do you do at...what's the company called again?" said Cho Cho, looking at Phillip.

"It's called "Head Hunters, damn Cho Cho, I been there almost three years!" said Phillip somewhat angry.

"Sorry," said Cho Cho.

"Well, that's exactly what I do" said Calder, "I'm a headhunter".

"So, what's that mean? You run around run around the city killing people and shrinking their heads?" Joked Cho Cho.

 Calder let out a sI'mple laugh.

"Yea, I string them up and hang them from my rearview mirror."

"Like fuzzy dice?" Laughed Robert.

"Like fuzzy dice." Echoed Calder.

"He finds companies that need to fill a specific position within there company." Said Phillip.

"And then I find the right person for them." Said Calder

"Didn't you guys buy a real shrunken head when you were in Borneo?" Asked Robert looking at Kayla.

"Yea" said Kayla, "we sure did, but they wouldn't let us bring it back into the country"

"Why not?" asked Robert

"Because it was someone's real fucking head!" said Kayla.

"Now we don't know that for sure." Said Cho Cho "But because they couldn't be sure it wasn't someone's real fucking head, they wouldn't let it through customs."

"Borneo" said Calder, "Wow, what took you two to Borneo?"

"Believe it or not, that's where we went for our honeymoon." Said Cho Cho.

"Your Honeymoon" said Calder "You two are married?"

"Six years now," said Kayla.

"Gees," said Calder, I thought you two were,"...He tried to catch himself but he couldn't stop his sentence. "gay."

"Now why would you think that." Said Kayla in a sudden serious tone, looking straight at Calder.

Calder felt his stomach tightening up a little as he tried to gather himself,

"Well, I don't know," mumbled Calder, "uh.. I guess, because, I'm ignorant."

"Yea," said Kayla, 'I guess you are."

An uncomfortable silence sat at the table for a second, while

Calder tried to think of something to say.

But then Calder continued.

"But you know, I don't have a problem with that," Said Calder, trying to dig himself out of the hole.

"I mean, I'd rather be ignorant than stupid. I've always felt ignorant just meant you didn't know, but still could learn. Whereas, being stupid meant you couldn't learn.

When someone is ignorant, there's always room for enlightenment."

There was another short pause at the table.

"Interesting perspective," said Robert. Breaking the silence.

Kayla was still thinking it over as the waiter showed up with the drinks, and not a moment to soon for Calder.

"So how long have you two been married? Asked Calder, desperately trying to change the subject. Oh, that's right six years. You just said that."

"What about you two? How long have you two been together?" Said Robert, pointing to Calder and Phillip.

"Oh, honey please," laughed Phillip. "I don't think so."

Calder almost choked on his beer,

"No, no no, we're not together. "I'm straight."

"Oh, then I still have a chance?" Asked Robert looking at Phillip.

"You already had your chance, said Phillip, "just be glad I'm still your friend."

Cho Cho and Kayla started to laugh as Cho Cho made the "shame on you" symbol with his two fingers at Robert.

Calder found himself dumfounded and a little confused by the outcome of the whole conversation. He drank his beer as fast as he could, trying not to look like he was guzzling it.

He was feeling embarrassed, but even worse, he was worried that he had embarrassed Philiip as well.

Fortunately, it never came up again in conversation. When he finished his beer, he said good night to everyone and went to the bakery to get his muffin. Unfortunately, by then the bakery was closed.

So Calder headed over to University Avenue to catch a bus up to Shattuck. He thought about walking home from there, but he was still feeling a bit bloated from guzzling that beer and he didn't feel like walking on a full stomach and having to deal with the homeless people on the street as well as the loud drunken college students crowding the sidewalks, so he jumped on the Bart.

When he got off at his exit, he was met with more of the same people he wanted to avoid. Pan handlers, kids skating in the Bart parking lot, guys playing congas, small groups of people in the shadows, smoking and drinking. The smell of weed floated in the air. He knew that Bart stations weren't exactly the most pleasant places to be after dark, unless you wanted to skate, pan handle, get high or play music. So he kept moving.

He was about a block from the Bart station heading home as the bay swallowed the last wave of sunset into the sea. He turned at a corner to cross the street. As he checked for cars, he thought about how the cellphone had turned so many humans into one dimensional (or what he called phone dimensional) creatures walking into the street, into traffic, completely oblivious of their surroundings as they focused completely on the little screen in their hands. As he waited for a car to pass, he noticed a man washing the dirt from his driveway, there were a pair of birds jousting for position on top of a light post, several boys walking down the middle of the street in the distance, an empty McDonalds bag tumbled down the street in the wind as a car passed as Calder finally crossed the street.

He was still a few blocks from home, when he heard the sound of faint voices from behind in the distance. He looked over his shoulder and saw what looked like the same group of boys he had seen earlier. But were they boys? They were a little closer now and appeared to be more like teenagers. And there was something about the tone of their voices, they way they were walking and posturing, something that seemed intimidating, and made him feel slightly nervous. Trying to ignore it he continued to walk home, but as he got closer to home, they got closer to him. He crossed the street just to change things up. He suddenly felt a need for distance between him and these boys. Walking under a large Japanese elm with its velvet white cups pointing up at the dark sky, he heard the boy's voices even closer, they had crossed the street as well. A pack of young boys making noise, the slap of rubber smacking on the wet street, or the screeching it makes on a basketball court. There were short vocal bursts, "Hey man" this and "what the fuck that" which only fueled his slowly growing anxiety. He stared walking a little faster, but in the dark he couldn't quite make out the undulating sidewalk being thrust up and down by tree roots busting from under the cement, and he started tripping and stumbling as the boys got even closer. "Hey dude" one of the boys called out. Fear started to take over. His heart started pounding and his fast walk suddenly became a quick jog. His place was just around the next corner, but the boys were almost on top of him now. "Hey mother fucker, come here" another boy shouted as Calder rounded the corner at a full run. Then bam! Sudden Impact, a pair of glasses smashed into his forehead as he ran smack into someone walking the other way on the street. They both crashed to the ground violently as keys and coins scattered about them. Their bodies bounced hard on the sidewalk and, skidded to a halt. The boys ran by without even noticing the collision. "Hey mother fucker, wait up" yelled one of them in another direction as they all ran off into the night as the two bodies laid on the cold Berkeley sidewalk.

"Oh shit," said a voice, "what happened, are you alright?"
Calder glanced over in a daze trying to focus.

Yea," I think so," said Calder, he could feel bits of gravel embedded in his palms. "I'm so sorry, are you okay? "Well, I think so, but let's take stock,"

As they both started to get up and check out the damage, the woman noticed one of her shoes about three feet away, her glasses were laying between his feet. Calder slowly rolled up on to his knees and brushed his hands together to get the gravel out of his skin.

"Geez, I'm really sorry," said Calder, "I hope you're okay."
"Why were you running like that?" The woman asked.
"I thought somebody was chasing me," said Calder
"What? Who?"

"But I was wrong, I'm sorry," said Calder, "I guess I got scared, never saw you coming, but are you sure you're, okay? It looks like you're elbows bleeding."

The woman looked at the blood on her elbow.

"No," she said, "I don't think that's me."

Calder suddenly felt a warm, sharp pain in his forearm. Blood slipped through a clean tear in the sleeve of his jacket.

"Looks like I got you," she said as she held up her left arm.

Her left arm had a prosthetic hand that had a hook on the end that was covered with blood.

Surprised he hadn't noticed her prosthetic arm and feeling the pain of the wound had Calder's head slightly spinning.

"That's bleeding pretty good" she said, "We should look at it"

"No, it's ok, I live right here," said Calder picking up her shoe and handing it to her.

She put it on and grabbed her keys off the sidewalk as Calder retrieved his change.

"Look, I'm really sorry," said Calder, "If you have any injuries or pain from this just let me know and I'll…"

"No, no, I think I'm ok" she said as she noticed a few drops of blood on the sidewalk. "But I would feel better if we looked at that, you should know what you're dealing with,"

Calder pulled his arm out of the jacket. The blood had already stained the whole forearm of his shirt. He pulled up his sleeve to expose a deep gash.

"Well, that can't feel good," she said, "sorry bout that."

"No, no, it's all my fault. I'll be ok, I got a roll of gauze, I'll wrap it up, it'll be fine." Said Calder

She took his wrist in her hand and turned his arm to the streetlight as they stood in the dark. Calder looked at her face as she examined his arm. She seemed focused in her inspection.

"If you wrap it with gauze, it will probably heal, but you'll have an ugly scar. Stitches would be better and less chance of infection."

"What are you, a doctor?" He asked.

"Not quite, I'm a nurse at Alta Bates."

"Really"? asked Calder.

He thought about the odds of being cut by a nurse with a prosthetic hand.

"Well, I don't want to go to Alta Bates."

"Well, maybe you don't have too," she said. "I think I could patch you up with some things I got at my place. I live right here too. You wanna let me patch you up? It's the least I could do after cutting you open"

Calder didn't really hear anything after she said, "I live here too" He suddenly recognized this woman as the woman from across his courtyard. From that moment on, everything felt like a hazy dream. He felt himself in a daze as he followed her up the stairs to her apartment. The same apartment that he had stared at so many times through his window across his courtyard from his apartment. He couldn't believe it. Now what were the odds of that!

As he followed her up the stairs to her apartment, he recognized her silhouette as it blocked out the lights shining down the stairwell. She was talking over her shoulder as they walked down the hallway. He could hear kids giggling and screaming from behind a door as they passed one of the apartments.

"Can you wait outside a second while I get you a towel, the last thing I need is blood on my carpet, I just vacuumed."

As she opened the door, Calder made one last protest.

"Really you don't have to do this, I live right across the..."

"Hey, it's my job" she said as she started to close the door, but left it slightly ajar and peeked back through the narrow opening. "I'll be right back" she said as he got a quick peek at her pair of brown eyes and a nose ring before she disappeared into the apartment calling back, "Don't let the cat out"

He stood there in the hallway with is arm bleeding looking at her door. He could still hear the kids playing in the distance from the other apartment. For a second, he thought about just going back to his place and leaving a thank you note on her door the next day. But then he heard a meow. He thought the cat might be coming for the door. What if the cat tried to get out? He pictured the cat trying to run out the door and him trying to close it. That could be bad, catching its head or ribs in the door jam as it screeched and squirmed trying to get out or back into the apartment. If he knelt down and tried to stop it with his hands, he could get scratched to shit! His arm was now starting to throb, he felt a painful lump on his head and it felt like someone had hit him in the hip with a hammer. He was pretty banged up and pretty confused.

He had just run into a woman, and knocked her so flat to the ground that her shoe had flown off. And yet he was standing in front of her apartment door waiting for her to come and patch his wounds. Why would a woman take a stranger, who out of the blue knocked her so flat that she came out of her shoe, take this stranger back to her apartment to bandage him up? The door opened. She had a small towel in her hand. She wrapped the towel around his forearm.

"Here, try this." she said, "Put your hand over it and come into the kitchen,"

He followed her into the kitchen, where he noticed the poster of all those tomatoes hanging on the wall.

"Put your arm over to the sink" she told him, "and let's have a look at it."

She unwrapped the towel and pulled up his sleeve. A nice clean slice, shaped like a blood red smile stared back up at Calder. She poured some hydrogen peroxide over the wound. The hydrogen peroxide bubbled up and fizzed as it ran into the cut and down into the sink. She took a good look at it.

He took a good look at her looking at his cut.

"By the way, I'm Calder" he said.

She rolled her eyes realizing they hadn't yet introduced themselves.

"Oh shit," she said looking back at him. "I'm sorry, I'm Lou."

"No, no, I'm the one who's sorry here...I mean, I ran into you," said Calder, "and now I'm here, in your home and..."

There was an awkward silence for a second or two.

"Well, It looks like about eight stitches," said Lou

"I can do it right now, if you like. Or you could go to Alta Bates, if you feel better doing that."

Calder tried to assess his situation. Here he was in a strange house with a stranger, who was about to stitch up his arm, yet it felt familiar. He didn't like his assessment. She didn't know he had seen the poster before, or that he had seen the sofa with its red paisley print. She didn't know, that he knew, if he looked over his shoulder he would see the vacuum cleaner in the corner against the wall. She didn't know that he already knew when he came into her apartment that there was a cat in the house. Calder felt like he had a shameful secret.

Maybe it was the rush of adrenaline he was having from actually being in the apartment that he had looked at from across his courtyard, standing next to the woman he had only seen in shadow and silhouette. Or maybe it was the same rush he felt when his dad turned off the headlights of the car in the dark night speeding down a dark road. That sense of fear and exhilaration, and risk, all at the same time. Then he noticed that some of the framed photos on the wall. Some were photos of her in nurse scrubs with other nurses and doctors, some looked like framed college degrees with medical symbols. And for the first time he felt himself breathing. So he decided to turn off the headlights of the car in his head, and take a risk, and accept her offer

"Well,, I don't want to wait in a waiting room for three hours to get eight stitches."

He placed his arm over the sink and decided to be brave. Lou pulled over a box that looked like a very professional first aid kit and tackle box all in one. She flipped it open like she'd done it a thousand times, which eased Calder's nerves a little more. She picked out a surgical glove with her hook and slipped her hand into it and then poured more hydrogen peroxide over her prosthetic hook.. Then she pulled out tweezers, thread, needles and a couple different bottles of liquid, as Calder watched. He was amazed how well her prosthetic hook worked as effortlessly as her other hand. Threading the thin needle, folding open squares of gauze, opening a bottle cap and pressing the gauze into the top of the bottle and soaking up the liquid inside.

She placed the wet gauze on his cut for about a minute. He couldn't help but notice the concentration and yet ease and familiarity she displayed. As they waited for the liquid in the bottle to take affect, he felt the cat rubbing against his ankle.

He looked down.

"That's Turk, he's trying to help you relax." said Lou.

"Oh really"? said Calder.

"When the people in your building know that you're a nurse, you get a lot of kids with cuts and bruises that need attention. Turk helps them relax while I patch them up"

She took the thin needle and lightly poked the area around his wound,

"Feel anything?" Asked Lou.

"Not a thing," said Calder.

"Well, then you can watch me stitch you up, or you can watch Turk, whatever makes you comfortable."

Calder did both.

For the next twenty minutes he watched the hook that had cut him open, hold his arm delicately by his wrist as she worked on his cut. He watched the cat pace back and forth between his ankles, purring as it rubbed against his calves. He watched her bend slightly forward turning her head to get a better angle with the needle. He noticed the slim blonde dreadlocks flowing out from under the scarf on her head and draping the back of her neck. The coral blue earring dangling from her ear lobe. The small soft golden hairs on her neck under the earring that was sharing the space with a few soft faint freckles. He wondered how he had missed the prosthetic arm when he had watched her from across the courtyard. Then realized why the vacuum cleaner had looked so strange from his window when she was using it. The sharp point of the needle slipped through his skin on one side of the cut, then back out the other side coming up through his skin completely painless. As she slowly started to close the open wound, the tip of her tongue slipped through her teeth against her upper lip as she concentrated on her task. It was cute and Impressive at the same time.

As she got close to finishing the last few stitches, she unconsciously began humming to herself.

The song was ship of fools by The Doors.

"You like the Doors?" asked Calder

"Yea. Do you?" Replied Lou.

"One of my favorite bands. I've got several of their albums." Said Calder ""

"Yea, I like their stuff too" said Lou.

She put a bandage over the wound and began putting her things away. Calder stood up like he was leaving the doctor's office. She said something about changing the bandage in a few days and keeping it clean. But he was noticing the tear in her sleeve, and the blood on her elbow.

"Looks like you gut a cut too."

Lou glanced down at her elbow.

"Oh darn, what the..."

She pulled up her sleeve and took a look.

"Oh, it's not that bad," she said, I'll can clean it up in the shower, not a problem"

She looked back at Calder, there was another brief silence as he stood there looking at her

"Well then," said Calder... "I guess I better get going, and uh..let you get on with your evening. You sure you're alright?"

"Yea," said Lou, "I'm fine. You might want to take some Tylenol or something to help you sleep. That arm's probably gonna hurt a bit when the numbing wears off."

"Will do." replied Calder, as he started for the door. "Can I give something for your time, and all this trouble?" He asked her.

"No, no. It was no trouble, it's good to practice my stitches."

As they got to the door, he turned to her.

Well, can I at least buy you a meal, lunch or something, maybe some dinner?"

She up at the wall, as if contemplating his suggestion, then looked back at him,

"Can I think about it"? She asked

"Yea, sure," said Calder, as he stepped out into the hallway. "Just let me know."

As she started to close the door, Calder looked back,

"But, how will you let me know?" he asked.

"Well," said Lou, "you're my neighbor right"?

"Yea, I uh, I live right next door," said Calder.

"Yea" said Lou, as she pointed to her window. "Your window faces mine across the courtyard, right?"

Calder felt a sudden lump in his throat.

"Yea" he said, "I guess your right"

"Well then, I'm sure we'll run into each other again, no pun intended."

They both let out a brief laugh.

"Fair enough." Said Calder as he headed down the hallway

Part of him was nervous from her pointing through her window across the courtyard straight to his window, and part of him slightly excited that she knew exactly where he lived.

14

He should've been looking at his watch, because he was running late. But he was looking at a dog chasing a ball. He should've been thinking about getting to the Bart on time. But as he headed to work, he was thinking about Lou. How she had patched him up after he smashed into her on the street as he ran scared in the night. He was thinking about the fear he had, that had him running like that when he thought he was gonna get beat up and mugged by a bunch of black teenagers. But it didn't matter what he was thinking. It didn't matter what he was watching. It didn't matter how late he was, because he wasn't going to make it to work today. He wasn't going to make it to work ever again.

As he approached the BART station, he saw several black cars in moving slowly down the street. Black and white motorcycles ridden by old men in black leather jackets rolled along the side of the cars in slow motion. He stopped and waited on the corner with a group of people as the procession took over the avenue. He watched the faces in the cars as they passed. Calder had ideas of slipping between the cars so he could make his Bart. But as he stepped into the street a rent a cop on a motorcycle waived him back to the curb, and he returned to the sidewalk.

The green funeral stickers flapped under the windshield wipers of the cars that rolled by. Solemn faces looking through the windows at the grey day, as the wheels of a hearse pushed water out of the potholes in the road. Calder stood there on the corner in a group of strangers on the street, watching a funeral go by, knowing he missed his train.

As the funeral moved along, Calder was looking out towards the bay and the city on the other side when he felt the vibration of his phone in his pocket. It was Phillip.

"Hi sweets, it's Phillip" he sounded somber.

"Look" said Calder "I'm running late, but the next train will be here in about..."

"Never mind that," interrupted Phillip. "There's been an accident and it's bad...Joshua is dead"

"What!" yelled Calder "Joshua's dead!"

"It was some kind of skiing accident in Whistler" explained Philiip, "His brother just called and gave me the news. He wanted your number. He said he'd call you in about an hour,"

Calder was flabbergasted, he put a finger over one ear so he could drown out the sounds of the street.

"Oh my gosh I can't believe this, this is terrible,"

"I know," said Phillip "I can't believe it either."

Calder tried to compose himself.

"Ok, look," said Calder "the next train is about 10 minuets away, I'll be at the office in about..."

"No, no, it's not happening." Said Phillip. "At least not today. His brother said we couldn't do any work at the office until they sorted things out. He was all business and to the point. You remember him, we met him once when he came by the office to look at the books. Alton or Ashley or something like that."

"Ashton," said Calder

"Whatever, he certainly didn't sound like his brother had just died," said Phillip angrily.

Calder thought about what he remembered about Ashton Meyer, and couldn't say he was surprised to hear that. The funeral procession had come to a momentary stop and blocked the street. Calder thought about what he should do.

"Well look, I'll come by the office and get a few things and we'll call the other guys and you and I will close up the place," he said to Phillip.

"Too late, I'm already in my car. Ashton told me to lock up the office and leave my keys with building security," said Phillip

"What? Wait a second, I've got my keys, I can get into the office," Said Calder.

"Calder, a friend of ours just died." Said Phillip in a sad voice, "I know he was really just our boss who paid us the for the work we did that made him a lot richer then we are, but he was a nice man. And although we rarely saw him, we liked him. I feel sad that he's dead. So, I'm gonna go home and drink the last of the Sapporo's that were in your fridge and I'm gonna have a toast to Joshua Meyer. I suggest you do the same thing."

Calder looked out again towards the bay. The funeral procession slowly started to move again. The sun reflected off the windshield of a car and caught Calder square in the face. It blinded him momentarily and he put his head down, and covered his eyes with his hands. Out of the blue he had a sudden flash memory of being in junior high with his buddies, and reflecting the sun off their watches and pointing the light in other kids faces. For some reason it made him smile and even laugh a little. But as his eyes started to water up from the glare, it felt like tears. Then he thought about Joshua being dead and actually started to cry. He backed up out of the crowd and tried to get his vision back. He sat against a wall for a second to breath.

The funeral procession moved on, and so did the crowd. Calder decided to take Phillip's advice, and head back home.

As he made his way towards home, he wasn't wondering about the irony of hearing about a friend's death at the same time he was watching a funeral procession go by.

He wasn't wondering why his emotions had him laughing one moment and in the next instant he was starting to cry.

As Calder walked home, he was wondering about the teenagers who he thought were chasing him. He was thinking he never really saw any of them. So why did he think they were black?

Back at his apartment, Calder decided to make something to eat. He was still trying to grasp the fact that Joshua was dead. He was feeling sad and frustrated. He was also feeling angry at himself for jumping to conclusions. Or in his case jumping to assumptions. After all, he had been raised by parents who had taught him not to judge people by the color of their skin. And yet he had done just that. He was mad at society for brainwashing him and so many others into racial profiling through the media. How throughout history racial propaganda had poisoned the ignorant and even seduced the intelligent into stereotyping races and cultures. This thought only fueled his sadness. But as he thought about it a little more, he was glad that he had reflected on his experience and that his ignorance was fighting off the poison and that his intelligence had not been seduced.

He had just finished making a tuna fish sandwich when his phone went off. It was Ashton. After a brief stale mention of the tragedy and family grief over the sudden death of Joshua, Ashton went right to business. He said the family had no interest in keeping the company and that Calder should clear out his office within the week and turn in his keys to security blah, blah, that his secretary will send him the last of his commission checks, blah, blah; how Joshua appreciated all the work he had done blah, blah blah, blah!

When Ashton finished talking, Calder hung up the phone. He had already stopped listening a while ago. He was too busy staring across the courtyard below at Lou's window. She was writing on it with white foam. Shaving cream or whipping cream or something like that. She was writing backwards so he could read it. It said, HOW'S THE ARM? He was Impressed by how effortlessly she wrote backwards. He thought for a second, then went into the bathroom and grabbed a bar of soap from the shower. He went to his window and using the soap like a piece of chalk, he did his best version of backward writing that he could, and managed to spell out the word FINE. He looked over at her window and saw her looking over at his. He saw her face looking at his. He raised his arm and gave her a gentle wave. She gently waved back, and then just stood there for moment looking back at him. Then she took her hand and smeared the foam in circles until it made her window all white, like when a store is going out of business. Then she took her finger and wrote through the white foam, LUNCH? Calder smeared the bar of soap up and down over what he wrote until his window was all white like when a store is going out of business. He used his thumb to scrape out the word YES through the soap on his window.

Maya slowly opened her eyes and stared up at the ceiling. She remembered hearing Paul drive off to soccer practice with the boys. She thought of the love they had finally made the night before, and a warm smile filled her face. The Art Deco chandelier slowly swayed above her in the soft wind that was coming through the window. The solar system represented in lights looking down from over their bed.

A round teal bulb representing the blue planet earth fell in line with a golden bulb representing the sun. A crescent shaped bulb, that would be hard to replace, represented the moon with Saturn and its rings getting into place. The rest of the bulbs took their positions and the solar system was aligned.

Paul saw the paper on the porch when he got back from soccer practice, so he figured Maya was still sleeping. So he made the boys lunch and went upstairs to check on Maya. To his pleasant surprise, He found his wife typing away at the computer.

"No more writers block?" Asked Paul

"I guess I just needed some good sex and some good sleep," said Maya.

"Well, that's great," said Paul, "I guess my cock broke the block"

"Very clever" said Maya, "Crude, but clever."

"Looks like my dick did the trick!"

"Okay," laughed Maya, "enough puns"

"No, wait," said Paul, "I got more. "

"Don't need them," said Maya as she turned around in her chair and looked at Paul. She had a sly smile on her face.

"I finished the book."

Calder sat at a small table at Karala with a pair of chopsticks in his hand, swirling raw salmon and rice in some soy sauce and ginger. Lou sat across from him sipping miso soup. He couldn't believe that after all this time, he was actually sitting across from the woman he had watched from across his patio.

"So, how'd you get the name Lou" asked Calder.

"It's short for Lauretta," she said.

"Interesting," said Calder.

"Well," said Lou, "when I was little I had a cousin who had kind of a lisp, and he couldn't say Lauretta, it would come out Lewetta. The kids would make fun of him, so he just started calling me Lou cause it was easier for him, and it just stuck."

"Got it" said Calder. Makes sense." Any other interesting things I should know about you Lewetta?"

"Well," said Lou, "I was in prison for five years"

"What! Really?" Asked Calder.

"Yea," said Lou, "I shot a man for beating his dog."

CPSIA information can be obtained
at www.ICGtesting.com
Printed in the USA
LVHW020325220222
711655LV00012BA/402

9 781662 840388